I0629322

THE SIGN OF FOUR

A Novel

Steve Herman

GRAVIER HOUSE PRESS
An Independent Publishing Company
New Orleans, Louisiana
1999

Library of Congress Publication Data:
Herman, Steve.
The Sign of Four / Steve Herman.
ISBN 978-1-7335181-2-3
(Original GHP Paperback ISBN 0-9671179-2-5)
Fiction.
Library of Congress Catalog Card Number: 99-95341.
© *Copyright by Stephen Herman, 1995.*

First Edition
September 1999

This book is a work of fiction. Names, characters, places and incidents are used fictitiously, and any resemblance to actual persons, living or dead, events, or locales, is entirely coincidental.

The customary legal admonition is: All rights reserved; printed in the United States of America; no part of this book may be used or reproduced without written permission, except in the case of brief quotations embodied in critical or scholarly articles or reviews. I think people have – and/or certainly should have – a little more freedom to quote or incorporate the works of others. But I would appreciate a formal request for permission, even if you think the intended application constitutes Fair Use. Queries regarding such rights and permissions should be addressed to Gravier House Press, Post Office Box 50337, New Orleans, Louisiana 70150-0337.

Excerpts from the following have been reprinted by permission: Lorando and Rose, "Reality and 'E.R.'" Times Picayune, March 30, 1995, p.E-1. Reprinted with permission of The Times-Picayune Publishing Corporation. All rights reserved. Charles Osgood, "The Osgood File" May 1995. Reprinted with permission of CBS Radio. All rights reserved. "Playboy Interview: Tom Cruise" Playboy, January 1990, pp.58-59. Reprinted with permission from Playboy, Inc. All rights reserved. The History of Philosophy by Julian Marias. Reprinted with permission from Dover Publications. All rights reserved. Acknowledgment is also made to Peter Laufer, Inside Talk Radio (Birch Lane Press 1995), Steve Rendall, The Way Things Aren't: Rush Limbaugh's Reign of Error (New Press 1995), and, of course, The Sign of Four, by Sir Arthur Conan Doyle (1890).

For Penny

While the individual man is an insoluble puzzle,
in the aggregate he becomes a mathematical certainty.

- Sherlock Holmes, <u>The Sign of Four</u>,
by Sir Arthur Conan Doyle, 1890.

CHAPTER ONE

"I'm gonna grab some lunch."

"Okay."

"You want anything?"

"No thanks."

"Okay, I'll see you in a little while."

"Wait a second."

"What?"

"You got anything planned?"

"No."

"What about the commercial fishing controversy?"

"Nah" I said. "Too provincial."

"I like to have things planned."

"I'll see you in a little while."

"Just so we can run a promo during the midday show."

"I'll find something, bye."

"Be back before three."

"Bye."

Andre was in the booth. She was interviewing a tall dark gentleman who was playing with a cigarette in his left hand and sipping coffee from a WWL 870 AM mug. His hands were tired and worn, with those little brown sun spots that develop over the years when you spend a lot of time on the water. My grandfather had those spots. He was a seaman from Greece, and they remind me of the Mediterranean.

Andre was dressed up today. She had one of those expensive suits from Petite Sophisticate with her Ebel watch and a silk Kandinsky scarf from Tiffany's. I think she was going to lunch at Commander's with one of the guys from Snapple after the show.

Outside the booth, my program manager was still sifting through newspaper articles and entertainment business magazines. We usually have morning conference calls. I would be at home watching the Today Show and reading the newspaper, and the producer would call me up from the station, and conference in Max, the program manager, and Mike, the engineer. We would kick around ideas, see what would work and how to handle it, what guests we might try to have, and how to make the topic interesting. But the last few days, our producer had been in Texas on a camping trip with her boyfriend, and the program manager was searching frantically for a topic. He liked to have things planned.

Max was a pretty good guy, all in all. He was short, and heavy, with these dark Italian eyes and this one yellow tooth that was third from the right. He was always tugging at the curls of his moustache, and parted his hair in the middle of his head like one of those Fred Flintstone bowling partners right out of the fifties that you sometimes see in barber shops or playing pool. Max was one of those guys that worked his way through college as a disc jockey for weddings and bar mitzvahs and sweet sixteen parties, spinning the records and the cds, and flirting with the girls. He got a masters in communications from UNO, and worked at WNOE for a while, before coming over here. His specialty is setting up everybody's home computer system. I think he spends a lot of time on the Internet, or America On-Line, or whatever, pretending to do research for the program, but really spending most of his time looking for dates.

In any event, I was starving, and went out into the reception area where Tonia, my secretary, was sorting out deliveries next to the little coffee table with four styrofoam cups and an empty box of doughnuts beside the automated

Mr. Coffee machine. I'm going to lunch, I told her, and went across the hall to the Offices of Edmund P. James.

"May I help you?" asked the receptionist.

"Could you tell Edmund I'm here please" I said, and he started to punch the extension number into the phone. I think his name was Fred or Alvin or something. He was one of those receptionists that gets very annoyed if you disturb them, while they are trying to do their nails, or play solitaire on the computer, or read their Anne Rice books, and whatever else it is that they do. This guy was flipping through an old antiques catalogue, and was particularly condescending. He had these tiny little eyes, with hair that was swept and maybe even moussed back over the side of his face, with red lips and a strange little nose. He had a high nasal voice, and was tapping his pencil with the Mickey Mouse eraser next to the phone.

The waiting room was small, and rectangular, with shelves of leather-bound books and hand-coloured architectural prints from DeVille's Print & Book Shop, which was just a few blocks away. Across from the receptionist were a couple of chairs and a little glass table with Harper's Bazaar and New Orleans magazines.

"Mister Wilson is here" the receptionist was saying, while I sat down in one of the chairs and opened up the March issue of Vanity Fair. I flipped past the Hennessy Martini ads and the Florence Cromer dresses to a gorgeous young mother (who was not really a mother) chasing her naked child on the beach. There was a red venetian Chopard Casmir ad which smelled like rubbing alcohol, and some photographs of Elizabeth Taylor through the years. I always thought she looked the best in Suddenly Last Summer, though some say Cleopatra or Cat On A Hot Tin Roof. There was a grandfather clock on the wall, which was ticking and tocking, and I looked at my watch, where the times were the same.

A few minutes later, Edmund exploded through the doorway. He was a big, gregarious fellow, kind of

Falstaffian, (though only in disposition), who rushed in saying hello Robert and gripping my hand.

"Hey, you wanna go over and grab some lunch?" I asked him.

"Sure, just come back to my office for a second" he said. "I've just got to finish up one small thing."

I followed him through the doorway, and into a white labyrinth of computer-rooms and laboratories, audio-video surveillance equipment, faxes, darkrooms, and copy machines. Several of his associates nodded to us as we passed by the various doorways, while Edmund was saying "I heard your show the other night about the diminishing coastline, and found it extremely interesting."

I thanked him, and followed him into his office, where the sun was coming down through the windows and onto the green warneckii leaves in the corner of the room. Edmund's office was draped with oriental sheets of silk that were really floor rugs even though they were hanging on the wall. He had these tiny ornaments displayed in cases with a collection of clocks and microscopes along with these tiny glass and jade or onyx figurines.

Edmund was wearing one of his seersucker suits, with white Dexter bucks, and an alabaster tie. He has these big rosy cheeks with blue eyes, and kinda looks like Cannon from the television series, with a thick neck and a bald spot over his brow. After showing me in, he went fumbling around in his desk for a minute or two. He was looking for something, and there was a lit cigar still burning in his tray.

"So where you wanna go?" he asked me.

"I don't know. I thought maybe we could go to-" "-excuse me, Mister James, a Miss Beverly Winston is here to see you."

"Let Michael take care of it" he said.

"We could go to Domilise's" I suggested. "You ever been there? They have a great hot smoked sausage and a really good roast beef and swi-" "-excuse me, I'm sorry to bother you again, but she will only talk to you. She says it's an emergency."

"That's okay" I told him, "I've got plenty of time."

"Show her in then" Edmund said. "Thank you." And then he apologized. That's okay, I assured him, I've got plenty of time.

When I looked up, Beverly Winston was standing in the doorway. She had short red hair, dark red, near brown, which was parted on the left and curled gently against her neck, just over the tailored collar of her dress. Her cheekbones were high, and full, with carefully blended rouge, and delicate tones. She had these mysterious green eyes, both hopeful and sad, with carefully painted lips and a bit of powder on her nose.

"Hello, Miss Winston" the detective said, "this is my friend Robert Wilson."

"Nice to meet you."

"Mister Wilson is somewhat of a celebrity in the city" Edmund added. "But I'm sure that is not why you have come."

"No" she said. "But it's nice to meet you anyway."

"Nice to meet you too" I said.

"Please, sit down, if that makes you more comfortable" said Edmund, taking a fresh stick of gum from his desk and offering a piece to his guest. But she didn't want any.

Miss Winston was dressed in a formal white suit, with ill-fitted gloves and a hat that dipped down hiding the edge of her face. Her nails were freshly painted. Red Royal, I think, by Chanel. Her lips were soft and quivering, and she appeared both anxious and shy as she hesitated before sitting in one of the chairs.

She looked around the office and took a cigarette case out of her purse. She was trying to hold one to her lips, but her fingers were nervous and the cigarette kind of just dangled around clumsily in her hand while Edmund obliged her by presenting instinctively a tarnished lighter from the top of his desk.

"Thank you" she said, lighting the cigarette and taking a quick puff on the filter before blowing the smoke out into the air. "The reason I came to see you, Mister James, is that my cousin said you helped her out a few years ago–she was getting a divorce–and she said that you were good."

Edmund nodded graciously.

"Gabrielle Marsh, was her name, at that time" said Miss Winston. "Now it's back to Gabrielle Sands."

"I remember her well."

"She moved to Santa Fe after the divorce" Miss Winston told him. "She's into Native American pottery... or something."

"What can I do for you, Miss Winston?"

"I guess I better start at the beginning" she said, and Edmund said I think that might be a good idea. "My father" she began, "wasn't really into the family thing. He was always running off around the world with a bunch of hair-brained schemes and half-baked adventures. My mother was a secretary at Lykes Brothers, and she took care of me. But she died when I was young, and so my grandparents shipped me off to a boarding school, where for the most part I was raised. In any case, when I was around sixteen, I got a telegram from my father. He was in South America at the time. I was excited at first, but then I forgot about it, until I received a really long letter, in which he apologized for leaving me. He told me that he loved my mother. And that he was going to be coming home for Christmas. And that he wanted to see me. He wanted to make it up to me."

Even though she was nervous at the beginning, her voice had this underlying beauty to it, kinda like a harp or a cello or something, so that her speaking was really more like a song. As she told us more and more of her story, the anxiety receded, and it was kinda like A Clockwork Orange, in the milk bar, when the opera singer chants the chorus of Beethoven's Ninth, like some rare bird of gorgeous form.

"He sent me an airline ticket" she was singing, "and told me to meet him on December 23rd at the Dauphine Orleans. When I got to the hotel, though, they told me that a Stephen Winston was registered there, but that he wasn't in his room. I waited all day and all night, and then the next day we called the police. They never found him. And as far as I know, no one ever heard from him again."

"And when was this?" Edmund asked, as he opened a notebook. "December twenty-third..."

"Nineteen eighty."

"Was there any luggage in the hotel room?"

"Nothing that seemed to interest the police. He had some clothes and a bunch of junk from somewhere in South America, Colombia or Brazil. The only thing he had of any value was a pocket watch, which I kept. I hocked it a few years ago when I got into a jam. But then I felt guilty, because it was the only thing of his that I had, so I saved up and got it back."

"Did your father have any close friends here in town, that you know of?"

"Just a guy named Frankel. I think his first name was Henry or Harry, or... Henry. That's it. Henry Frankel. Anyway, the police contacted him at the time. They had rummaged around in South America together a long time ago, but he hadn't heard from him in years. But anyway, back to my story, a few years after my father disappeared, there was an advertisement in the newspaper, looking for Beverly Winston, the daughter of Stephen. I didn't have an address in town because I was living in Washington, but my grandparents sent me the ad. They didn't want me to answer it—they thought it might be dangerous for some reason—but I was curious, so I answered the ad in the newspaper, giving my address in D.C. A few days later, I got this package, and in the package was an emerald necklace. Just in a box."

"Did it have any writing on it?"

"No, just a plain black box. I've got it right here." The woman took a small box from her pocketbook, which Edmund inspected with care. "I brought them to Adler's to have them appraised" she said, "and they're real. One to two carats a piece."

"They're beautiful" he said.

I agreed.

"Anyway, I don't know if any of this is really relevant. But I have a feeling that it is." Beverly stopped for a moment, and concentrated on her cigarette. Edmund went over to the window, and placed his fingers gently on the sill. "And you were about to tell us?" he said.

"What?"

"Relevant to what, Miss Winston?"

"Oh" she said, "I got a letter two days ago, at my house, in Baltimore." And she took a white envelope from her purse, handing it to Edmund. "It says that I am supposed to meet someone outside Longue Vue Gardens tonight at seven. I am scared to go alone, but I'm too curious not to go. And so, basically, that's why I'm here."

"Be at the entrance of Longue Vue Gardens in two days' time at seven o'clock in the p.m." Edmund read aloud. "You are a woman wronged. But justice will be done. You may bring someone with you if you are skeptical, but please, no police. If you contact the police, I will have to say no, and you will never hear from me again. I hope to see you soon. A special friend." Edmund turned the note over and examined the envelope. "Can I keep this, just for a day or two?"

"Sure" she said. "Keep it. I don't need it. I know what it says."

"Where are you staying?" I then asked her.

"Um, the Royal..."

"The Royal Orleans?"

"No, the other one."

"The Royal Sonesta."

"Right, the Royal Sonesta."

"That's a nice hotel" I interjected.

"Yes" she said, "it is."

"So, Miss Winston" Edmund asked her, "what are you going to do?"

She laughed, snubbing her cigarette, and saying "that's why I came to see you."

"Well, if it's my decision" said the detective, "I will pick you up at the Royal Sonesta at around quarter to seven. We'll see if we can find out what's going on."

"I can meet you here" she offered. "I'm meeting my grandmother for lunch, and I'm gonna be down here the rest of the afternoon."

"Sure" he said. "That'll be fine."

"Can you come too?" she then asked me. I was standing in the back of the room, behind her, near the doorway, and she turned around to look at me while she stood. "Mr. James has everything covered, I'm sure. But it never hurts to have another strong body along."

"Well, I don't really know what I could do" I told her, "but if you want me to, sure. I have a show at four, but I guess I could make it by a quarter to."

"It was a pleasure to meet you" said Edmund, taking her hand, "and we shall see you this afternoon."

Miss Winston thanked Edmund again for seeing her on such short notice, and then she thanked me too. I couldn't help but think that she was vaguely familiar. Not that we had actually met before, but that she was recognizable, from some other place and time. I pictured her in a number of different venues. There were train stations and law offices and beaches and nightclubs and seventeenth storey penthouse apartment rooms. She was fixing her hat as she fastened her pocketbook. For some reason, I told her to be careful, and Beverly Winston was gone.

CHAPTER TWO

She's beautiful, I told him, as we grabbed our sandwiches and soft drinks from the counter beside a box of change. She was just like Faye Dunaway in Chinatown, or Lauren Bacall in The Big Sleep.

"You can't let your judgment be affected by personal qualities" was Edmund's response. "A client, to me, is just a factor in a problem. Just like any other factor. It's a means to an end. If you're blinded by that, you'll miss the big picture. And then you won't be any good to anyone, including the client."

"I suppose that's true" I said, "in a way." I was taking the top layer of bread from my sandwich and pouring Tabasco sauce over the lettuce and the shrimp. But in ancient times, people thought that physical beauty was the mark of a good person. That he or she had been somehow touched by God. And if you were ugly, on the other hand, or if you suffered from some handicap or deformity, they thought that it was the mark of some tragic flaw in your character, or malignancy of the soul.

"Well all I can say" Edmund was saying, "is that the most striking woman I have ever met got the death penalty when she poisoned three little kids to get their insurance money, and the most disgusting looking of creatures is one of the most powerful men in town."

"But in this case – "

"Never make exceptions" he told me. "Exceptions disprove the rule."

"Yeah, well, this all seems pretty far-fetched" I told him. "Some guy sends her an emerald necklace. Father travels around the world searching for treasure. Come on. The guy's probably shacked up in some trailer park with a hooker in Tennessee. The emeralds are probably a gift from some guy that had a crush on her in high school, got married to a rich girl he knocked up in college, and thinks it's his own magical way of making good. The letter is probably from some perverted co-worker who's been stalking her for months, and this whole meeting at Longue Vue is probably just a charade."

"Well, you've certainly got an active imagination" Edmund told me. "But it's really too early to speculate. If you start to develop your theory before you have enough facts, you will invariably twist the facts to fit your theory, rather than your theory to fit the facts. The real point is" he said, "no matter how fantastic things might seem to us, they are very real to your beautiful young friend."

"But you can't let yourself become blinded by that" I replied. "Then you'll lose sight of the big picture, and you won't be any good to anyone, including Miss Winston."

Edmund ignored me, for the most part. "Did you take a good look at her clothes?" he said. "Her gloves were too big, and they didn't really match, and that dreadful cap just cries out of someone attempting to look very elegant, and not knowing quite how."

"She was beautiful" I told him. "That's all that I can say."

"Perhaps" said Edmund, "that is all that you can say. Perhaps not. For instance, I can say that the man at that table over there has been doing a lot of writing lately."

"And why is that?"

"Well, you see how shiny his cuff is for about five inches, but then, if you look further up on the sleeve, you can see where it's smooth around the elbow, where he would rest it, while writing, on the desk."

That's neat, I admitted, while Edmund was then saying that it was clear that my bathroom window was on the left side of the sink.

"How do you know that?"

"You shave every morning, correct?"

"Generally."

"And, at this time of year, you shave by daylight."

"Okay."

"So given the fact that your shaving becomes less and less complete as we get further back on the right side, and absolutely slovenly at the jaw, one is led to the inescapable conclusion that the light, and hence the window, is much better on the left-hand side."

He was right, of course. Edmund was always figuring out these types of things. One time he figured out that an engineer had worked his way through school doing manual labor even though he was dressed in a suit and had no callouses because his right hand was a little bit bigger and more developed than his left.

Another time he figured out that I had been trapped in the May 7th flood because the leather soles of my shoes had marks on them from where I was trying to get the mud off, even though it was a week later and the tops of the shoes had already been polished.

He kinda reminded me of a psychic. Maybe psychics, I was thinking, were just people who had amazing powers of observation. And deduction. What I don't understand is those psychics that are on television with Dion Warwick and the Psychic Friends Network who, according to the telephone commercials, try to guess about things that happened to you in the past. What good is that? I don't need to know what happened to me; I already know. And really, what's the point of knowing what's going to happen? What are you supposed to do, try to avoid what happens – which would make their prediction wrong – or just be prepared? I went to a psychic once, in the French Quarter, off behind Bella Luna. He just told me about myself. Which was very engaging and seemed to be very penetrating and profound at the time, but when I got home, I realized that what he said was so general that it could have applied to anyone.

In any event, we hadn't had time to go to Domilise's, so we went to a sandwich shop downtown. It used to be called Mumphry's, until a couple of years ago, when they moved it down the street a few blocks and renamed it B&G.

The restaurant was filled with downtown businessmen and business ladies, who flooded out of the warehouse and giant office buildings to grab some lunch and smoke a cigarette in the middle of the day. There was no line, per se. You have to just kinda yell out the order over the counter and hope that someone starts to prepare your food. I looked around the room, where the crowd was thinning out a little. A young couple was ordering grilled chicken sandwiches with no mayonnaise and diet soft drinks. In the corner a man was drinking alone.

"Did you notice the stationary?" Edmund was asking me. Italian, very expensive, he explained. "Now look at the handwriting" he told me, taking the note from his pocket. "Concentrate on the long letters. See the l and the t ? Rich people always differentiate their long letters from the small letters, however illegible their writing might otherwise be."

"Would you be interested in doing a show?" I asked him.

"A radio show?"

"Yeah, a radio show. People call in. They ask you questions. You answer them. It'll be fun."

"Yeah, that would be interesting" he decided. "But first things first. We've got to attend to Miss Beverly Winston, and the matter at hand."

Edmund was finishing a plate of french fries, dipping them into a puddle of catsup and a tiny mound of salt at the edge of his tray. He had a napkin tucked into his shirt, which he used to clean his hands, and then fixed his spectacles. He took a cigar from his pocket, offering it to me, and then placing it in the center of his mouth beneath his nose. He chewed it around for a while, searching for a match, and then finally lit the cigar. It smelled like a muggy apartment with raw sugar caked on the counter and a stack of old newspapers burning on the stove. Edmund sat back in his chair and started to puff away, while I turned my head and tried to avoid the smoke, listening to the women at the table behind us discuss Victoria's Secret lingerie.

"I would never wear that stuff" one of the women was saying. "Why not?" asked the other. "Their bras are really comfortable."

"Really?"

"Yeah" she said. "Not the ones with the bars. Those hurt. But just the normal ones."

"Have you ever worn one of those – what do you call them – wonderbras?"

"I don't think so" she said. "Is wonderbra a name, like a brand, or is it just a kind of a bra that's made by a bunch of different companies?"

"I don't know" confessed the pretty one. "Maybe it started out like as a brand, and then that became the generic term. Like kleenex, or xerox, or coke."

"I don't know" she said, "I've never seen one."

"Neither have I."

"So, do you think that whoever sent the note is really a danger" I asked Edmund, "or do you think he just wants to give her something?"

"Well, you never know what people's ulterior motives are, but if I had to guess, I would have to say that whoever sent the note probably really wants to help her."

"Why do you say that?" I asked him, "besides the fact that someone sent her the necklace in the past."

"Because if you want to hurt someone, you just do it. It doesn't make any sense to go around creating evidence, or leaving clues."

"Yeah, but who ever accused criminals of doing things that make sense."

"Yeah, that's a good point" he said. "But actually I think that criminals are generally just about as rational in their methods as anybody else. They're just misguided in terms of their goals."

"I guess so" I said. That sounds reasonable. "It's a different kind of intelligence."

"Plus, maybe this special friend to Miss Winston wants to create evidence" he was thinking. "Maybe he wants to create suspicion."

"Why?"

"I don't know" he said. "Maybe he wants to frame someone else."

"Well, in any event, I've gotta get ready for the show." I waved off Edmund's cigar smoke, and threw the crunched up napkins onto my tray.

"Does it require a lot of preparation?" Edmund asked.

"Nah" I told him. "It's mostly just a matter of keeping up with everything that's going on in the world. While you're on the air, it's mostly just managing the time."

"There is a lot of pressure to stick to a schedule, go to commercial break and all that?"

"Some shows are more structured than others" I told him. "A lot of it depends on whether we have a guest. When there's no guest, I like to play it like the San Francisco 49ers. I script out the first fifteen plays or so, and then improvise from there."

"I listened to your program a few days ago – I think I told you. I was really impressed with the way that you took all of the issues, and then all of the sudden they were kind of like segregated and defined."

"Yeah, well, I was a philosophy major in college" I told him. Philosophy and communications. With a minor in film. "Then you know all about the philosophy of the butterfly" Edmund was saying. What's that? I asked him.

"Those who once were worms are soon to be angels" he told me. "But only for a week, and then they die."

CHAPTER THREE

"Billy from Destrahan, you're on the air."

"Yeah, Bobby, you know they fried that guy last night."

"Oh yeah, Michael Ward, did they execute him?"

"Yeah."

"The last I heard, they were waiting to hear from the Supreme Court."

"Nah, they killed him."

"When I went to sleep, he had just denied his last meal."

"Yeah, well, I guess if you are gonna die in a few hours, you're probably not gonna be all that hungry."

"That's pretty much a shame, don't you think? It's probably the only good food you get in the last ten or fifteen years of your life. And then you can't even eat. You know? They should probably give you your last meal a week or two before you are scheduled to die, so that you can actually enjoy it."

"Well that's cuz they keep those guys up there so long" the caller said. "Like that last guy, a couple weeks ago, that got stayed, he's been up there for like sixteen years, and he got to have his last meal before it got stayed."

"Really?"

"Yeah, it was like the six or seventh last meal the guy had."

"That's your tax dollars, buddy."

"Yeah, these guys been havin more steak dinners than me the past few years."

"Take care, man. Thanks for the call."

I have found that there's really no point in having any kind of a serious discussion about the death penalty. People will tell you that they're for it or against it because it's a deterrent, or because it's cost-effective, or not cost-effective, or because it's unreliable, or racist, or arbitrarily imposed. But really, when you get down to it, people who are for it are for it because they believe that if you kill somebody, you deserve to die, and the people who are against it believe that it's just plain wrong to kill anyone, and it's not society's place to judge. It's not really a political issue. It's a matter of psychology. And you're never really going to change anybody's mind. "Mason, from uptown, you're on the air."

"Hey Bobby, love the show."

"Thanks. What can I do for you?"

"I wanna talk about these old people."

"Okay" I said. "And don't lower your radio."

"What?"

"Yeah, turn it up as loud as it will go."

"Yeah, yeah, yeah" the guy was saying. "All right, okay, it's down" the guy said, but it was still too loud. "I wanna talk about the old people."

"Okay."

"I'm from Los Angeles."

"Yeah?"

"And they are the worst drivers. They should be put to sleep at the age of sixty-five."

"Okay."

"And second of all, when we go to the buffets, they are always getting in the way, stabbing you in the back with their plates, and stepping on your toes."

"Look, this is stupid" I told the guy. "I give a legitimate reason for getting rid of old people, and you start talking about stabbing you in the back with their plates. Come on.

There are plenty of young people that drive bad. Martha, from Houma, you're on the air."

The booth was small and plastic, with three guest chairs on the other side of an oval table and four large microphones. I was behind the table, in the corner, with a red WWL 870 AM sign over my head and a stack of control panels next to me on the floor. I had my little black and white television set in the corner, with the phone lines and a personal computer screen. There was a window next to me, on the left, where I could see the concrete parking lot and cars beside the Superdome. The sunlight was slanting down over the Poydras Street office buildings, and making its way over the busy streets below.

My producer would sit outside the booth, answering the phones and punching the information into the computer, so that I could see who was calling, where they were calling from, how long they had been waiting, and what they wanted to say. The engineer stood behind the control panel, which was this huge console of sound mixers and regulators, with reel-to-reel tape decks, computers, cd players, and microphones. Max was sitting in for my producer, who was still on vacation. I took a sip of coffee while responding to the caller, and picked up a paper-clip, starting to unfold it with my thumb.

"Jim, from Chalmette, you're on the air."

"Am I on?"

"Yes, this is Robert Wilson, you're on the air."

"Yeah, Bobby, I'm goin to Emeril's tonight with the wife. What should I get?"

"I don't know. Call Tom Fitzmorris."

"He said get the specials."

"Well, get the specials."

"Dude, if I'm gonna drop a c-note on dinner, I'm not gettin no specials. Specials is what they ordered too much of, last week, and want to unload. I wanna get something I know is gonna be good."

"Uh" and I stalled for a minute, thinking. "I think I got a porkchop there that was good."

"Porkchop?"

"Yeah, like a double-cut porkchop with some kind of a good sauce."

"That sounds good."

"Well, have a good meal."

"Thanks."

"Sure."

"Hey Bobby?"

"Yeah?"

"You ever watch Emeril on the Cooking Channel?"

"Yeah, he's funny."

"'Turn it up a notch!'"

"Bam."

"Take it easy Bob."

"Have a good meal." Of course, if he really wanted a good porkchop he could have gone to Lola's for half the price. But I guess it's not the same. "And we are talking about the death penalty, the budget, social security, environmental regulations, and – what the hell – porkchops. The customer's always right. Right? Just ask Michael Douglas in Falling Down. And Jeff, from Mid City: 'Kick it up a notch.'"

"Yeah, Bobby, I just want to say that, the thing is, that these guys write all these laws up there, in Washington or in Baton Rouge or whatever, and no one ever really knows what these things actually say. I mean, you got this guy saying it's a cut, and then you got some guy on the other side of the aisle saying it's not a cut, it's just a reduction in the annual increase. And it's like even if you do know who's telling the truth – if either one of them is – then still, no one short of a rocket scientist can figure out what the hell they are talking about."

I didn't say anything for a few seconds. I couldn't tell whether the guy was done. And just when I was about to respond, the guy started talking again:

"And so, you gotta depend on them to tell you what the ins and outs are, and they're all out to help their own side. I mean look at New York, is the perfect example. You got Moynahan on one side, and D'Amato on the other. How are you supposed to figure out what the heck is goin on?"

"You're right, Jim, what can I say. Probably, when it gets down to it, these guys don't even know what they're voting on. They're all relying on pages and aides and stuff, lobbyists, or other congressmen. All of the information is second hand. It's coming to them second hand, and so by the time it gets to you, generally through the media, it's fourth-hand or fifth-hand. And so, I think, as I've said before, that a more direct species of democracy is coming, where the lawmakers merely propose the laws, and the people actually vote on them, whether it's through the phone lines or whatever. And this will eventually force them to make the laws as simple, and direct, as possible."

"You think so?"

"I do. But the problem is: When that happens, then you're gonna have the opposite danger, which is that the most simplistic, slogan-like, bumper-sticker measures pass, even if, upon further analysis or reflection, that's really not what's best for the country. But that's the risk you take I guess, and until then...."

A guy named Wayne, from Gretna, wanted to talk about the environment. He had been waiting for 7 min. 42 sec. Fifteen minutes was about the average. We must have been having a light day of callers that day. "Wayne, from Gretna, you're on the air."

"Yeah, Bobby, back to what that lady was saying about all the regulations?"

"Yeah?"

"I'm usually conservative. But about the environment, I think that we have learned from the past, and just from common sense, it's become apparent, that corporations will do everything possible to make money. I mean, they will push it as far as it will go. And I'm just saying that, you know, I want my kids and my grandkids, god-willing, to have clean air, and clean water, and a place to play. So...”

I wasn't sure if he was finished, but it didn't sound like anything else was coming. “I like how you have that disclaimer at the beginning” I told him. “I'm usually a conservative. It's like, god forbid that anyone think you were anything but conservative. We wouldn't want that to happen. But the question is, is that really conservative?”

“What?”

“Getting rid of regulations about the environment. Is that conservative? I know it's Big Business. I know it's Republican. But is it conservative? Because I don't think that it is.”

“Well, I think it's conservative, in terms of economics, because it's kinda like the same thing as lay – what's that word? It's kinda like lazy fair.”

“Laissez faire?”

“Yeah, laissez faire. Isn't that conservative?”

I don't think so. “I mean, the terms liberal and conservative refer to philosophies about the nature of government. The liberal being someone who has the fundamental belief that people are inherently good, and that, left to their own devices, have the ability, in general, to govern themselves. It goes back to the Innocent and Noble Savage, and Rousseau. Conservatives, on the other hand, tend to believe that people are basically flawed – it pretty much stems from the idea of Original Sin – and so, to them, the government is there to protect people from each other, and really, to protect people from themselves. But where it gets confusing is that the two-party system that we have here in America really revolves around issues, not beliefs. And the perfect example is the right to bear arms. I mean, we think of that as being a very conservative idea, because the NRA and all of those groups have traditionally been members of the Republican Party. But if you think about it, the right to bear arms is a very liberal idea. Because conservative thinkers, like Edmund Burke for example, wanted to avoid any kind of anarchy or revolution at all costs, and therefore believed that a nation's arms should be concentrated in the hands of the government, to preserve the status quo.

"Liberals, on the other hand, like our Founding Fathers, believed in decentralizing the military, and placing physical power, as well as political power, in the hands of the people. To protect people from the tyranny of an oppressive government, and with the belief that ordinary citizens could be trusted to carry arms. It's just like this idea that liberals favor a strong federal government, while conservatives argue for states' rights. Because when you're talking about the EPA, for example, the Republicans want to decentralize the system, and give all the power back to the states. But when you're talking about litigation, they want to take the power away from the states, and create a uniform federal system. So when a company breaks the law, it's a local issue. But when it hurts someone, and he tries to sue the company, then it becomes a matter of national concern. So it's not really that the Republicans or anybody else is concerned with states' rights or any political philosophy; they just want to achieve a desired result. In the case of the EPA, they want to get rid of it, and in the case of the tort system, they want to insulate big business from suit. See what I'm saying?

"And so I think the environment is one of those issues where things get turned around. You don't trust the chemical companies, so you want government to put limits on what they're doing. That's conservative. The Republicans want to trust the companies to do whatever they want. That's liberal. And we need to be conservative about the time. Because it's almost out. And so anyway, thanks for the call. We gotta get out of here. See you tomorrow at four, right here, on news talk and sports radio, WWL 870 AM."

CHAPTER FOUR

Edmund was carrying an envelope when he stepped off the elevator. I was eating a bag of Charles potato chips and drinking a coke. I offered the bag to Edmund, who placed a couple in his mouth, and adjusted his spectacles. "Well, there really isn't any great mystery to this" he told me.

"You mean you've cracked the case already?" I asked him.

"No" he said, "but I have discovered something."

"What's that?"

"Henry Frankel died on the 28th day of April, 1984."

"So what?"

"Stephen Winston disappears, in New Orleans, in 1980. The only person he knew in New Orleans, at least according to Beverly, is Henry Frankel, who tells the police at the time of the disappearance, that he never knew that Winston was ever in town. Four years later, Frankel dies, and within weeks our young lady friend receives an emerald necklace anonymously through the mail. Now Miss Winston gets another anonymous letter which informs her that she is a woman wronged. Obviously, someone close to Frankel knows that he was somehow responsible for Winston's death, and wants to repay her in some way."

"I think you are letting your imagination get the best of you."

"Do you have any alternative hypotheses?"

"No" I said, taking another potato chip, "but, to use your own admonition against you, the facts seem twisted to fit the theory. For example: Why would the guy, or woman, or whoever, wait almost ten years to send the letter, and instead send some mysterious necklace? It makes more sense to think that her father is still alive. He feels guilty. And he doesn't want her to hate him. So he is taking on some strange identity. Pretending to be some long lost friend."

"And what will he hope to accomplish?"

"Her love. If he comes home and says 'Here I am, your father, sorry I missed out on the last thirty years of your life,' she is going to hate him. But if he comes back with some wild fantastic story about how he knew her father, and how he was a great man, who spoke of her often, and entrusted me with this necklace, that he saved for her, and all that, she will love him. Maybe not as a father. But as someone else. He will have her love. And maybe he doesn't even want that. Maybe he just needs it to get something else. Maybe he wants the necklace back. Maybe he needs to hide out for a while. Maybe he needs a place to stash some goods for a while, until the heat dies down. Maybe he's old and tired, and wants her to take care of him."

"I think you are letting your imagination get the best of you" he said. "There's just no reason..."

"But people aren't reasonable."

"Yes, well," the detective said, folding the envelope into his coat pocket, "we soon shall see."

We waited there for a few minutes. My hands were all greasy and salty from the potato chips. I threw the empty coke can into the trash, and started to wipe them off on my jeans. Then the elevator door opened, and Beverly stepped into the hallway. The first thing I saw were her eyes, which seemed kinda nervous and sad. I noticed that her lipstick had the slightest imperfection on the left side, under her nose, and the color of her face was kind of faded and pale.

She was wrapped in a beautiful dark brown top coat, with her arms folded protectively about her breast.

We stepped onto the elevator, where some fairly pedestrian saxophone music was funneled in over the door. "What do you know about this guy Henry Frankel?" Edmund asked Beverly, as I attempted to ask her if she ate anything interesting or got any good shopping done before she came. "He was pretty close to my father" she said. "They were in Bolivia together, or Colombia, one of those places. Maybe Brazil."

Maybe they were dealing drugs, I suggested. But Beverly didn't seem to take offense. "I don't think so" she said plainly. "My grandparents didn't think too much of my father, but they did mention a few times that he hated things which poisoned the body. When it came to alcohol, they said he never touched a drop."

We stepped off the elevator and into the lobby. There were a few late evening shoppers coming out of the stores with Wolf's Camera and Lord & Taylor bags. We cut through the men's department where all the ties were folded neatly on circular tables, and then through the jewelry department and all the rows of baby clothes. We went out of the Poydras Street exit, and Edmund hailed a cab.

"Longue Vue Gardens, please" he said to the driver, and held the door for me and Beverly.

"So, how was your afternoon?" I finally got a chance to ask her.

"It was pretty nice" she said.

"Did you eat anything interesting, or get any good shopping done before you came?"

"Nah" she said. "We had a pretty good lunch at this place called the Bon Ton and my grandmother bought a few things."

"That's nice."

"Yeah" she said, "it was."

The floor of the taxi was covered with newspapers. There was a Cellular One ad in the corner, with a Big Business Wins Big On Billiot Bill With Trick Play article and a dirty picture of John Hainkel, pandering for contributions. A sheet of bullet-proof plastic separated the front from the back seat, except for one of those rectangular cylinders near the bottom, where you and the driver could exchange money and change. The driver was wearing a light blue t-shirt and a navy Hawaiian. He set the initial fare to $1.50 and turned down the radio.

"What are you listening to?" I asked him. He was listening to the Howard Stern evening re-broadcast on 106.7 THE END. "Hey, you're Bobby Wilson" the driver then realized, examining my face in the rearview mirror. "I love the show, man."

"Thanks."

"I recognized you from that Dixie ad" he said. "On tv."

"You do tv ads too?" Beverly was asking, as the driver said "listen to your show, man, every day. Swear to god."

"Thanks" I said again, "I appreciate it."

"All the boys, I tell em, listen to Bobby, man. Bobby Wilson, he's the best."

"Even better than Howard?"

"Oh yeah" he said. "Howard aint got nothin on you."

The driver was kind of an Ignatius P. Reilly fellow. He looked like he was wearing a few drops of chili on his t-shirt, and had the smell of onions and relish on his breath. He was telling me how much his passengers love me, and how he always makes it a point of listening to the show. Meanwhile, Beverly was searching through her handbag. "When my father disappeared, in his hotel room" she was explaining, "there was a mysterious piece of paper that no one could understand. I don't think it's probably that important, but I thought you might want to take a look at it anyway."

"Hmn, it looks Indian" said Edmund. "See this hole. It's been pinned to a board."

"What is it?"

"It looks like a diagram of a building" he said. "See the halls and passages. It looks like a treasure map. See the cross."

"Three-point-seven from left. What does that mean?"

"Three point seven meters to left of this point, it looks like."

"What's that in the corner there?"

"It's some type of hieroglyphic or something" he said. "It looks like a swastika. The Sign of Four. Arturo Picon, Jaime Jimenez, Paulito Yzaga, Jonathan Small."

The symbol above the names did look like a swastika, and I started to think that maybe some kind of an Aryan or white supremacist group was somehow involved. A lot of Nazi death camp officers apparently fled to South America after the war, like in that movie The Boys From Brazil.

But the swastika was a symbol of ancient origins, which was considered a good luck charm by the druids and by Buddhists, and in medieval times, served as an emblem for the wheel or the cycle of life. The four arms represented the four winds, with the immobile heart at the center. It was even used in some cultures as a symbol of Christ.

"I don't know what it means, Miss Winston," Edmund was saying, "but it's obviously something that was important to someone. See, it's been kept in some kind of folder or a safe."

"How did you know that?"

"It was in a briefcase when we found it" said Beverly.

"Because both sides are equally clean" Edmund, at the same time, explained.

"That's amazing."

"You should hold on to that, Miss Winston" he told her, "we may need it later. I think this matter might be a lot more complicated than I first suspected."

The taxicab was winding down Metairie Road beside the golf courses and the catholic cemeteries, as the streetlights were softly reflected in Beverly's eyes. There was something musical and hypnotic about them. Something compelling and rare.

The hollow of her throat was strong, and pronounced, and she had one of those upper lips that was fixed in a permanent kiss. Her legs were muscular and elegant, and descended gracefully into a pair of sling-back heels that covered her toes. She was looking off into the distance, probably thinking about her father or a stalker or a bunch of diamonds or something, while her hands kind of fumbled around nervously in her lap. She was wearing one of those silver charm bracelets, I noticed. It had a fox, and a Ψ, and an owl. And whenever she turned her hands over in her lap, the figures would rattle against one another like a set of little triangles or bells. I put my arm on her shoulder, telling her that everything will be okay. She said thanks, and smiled, but seemed a thousand miles away, though, and so I started paying attention to the radio.

"But you saw that woman" Howard was saying. "She was like, *'Johnny Cochran wears the nicest suits. He is so fine. That Johnny Cochran... mm, mm, mm. A black man fine as he is dressed up like that could not lie. Christopher Darden, he's a race traitor. That's what he is. How's it gonna look if Mister Johnny loses this case? Huh? You tell me that. Representing a black man, who's a representative of this community, who played football for the Buffalo Bills, of Buffalo.'"*

"Well did you see that story in the National Enquirer," Jackie was saying, "about how the police never pursued another suspect, or any other possibility? And meanwhile the National Enquirer spent a million dollars trying to find any lead they could possibly cling on to."

"They were running down the four Colombian drug dealers angle, who came to kill Nicole and Fay Resnik, because they were scared that these two Beverly Hills housewives were going to take over the cocaine cartel."

"The housewife cartel."

"Right. So they came to kill them, and of course Fay wasn't there – she was in rehab – so they killed Nicole. And now all the housewives in Los Angeles are shaking in their boots, because they were thinking of taking over the cocaine cartel. So Rick Dees is making a fool out of every disc jockey that ever lived. I hate that guy. Right back. We've gotta take a break."

"Whatcha think about this Rick Dees fella, Mister Wilson?" asked the cab driver.

"Howard's right" I told him, "the guy's a ted."

"I think so too, Mister Wilson. I never liked that guy. Kasey Kasum neither. I never liked any of those left coast guys. They're all a bunch of hippies out there. Hippies and gays."

In radio, the trick is kind of appealing to everyone by appealing to no one. You do what interests you, and hope that it's interesting to others. Sure, you can do some market research and target studies and polling and ratings and all of that. But how are you going to construct a show that is designed to appeal to both the cab driver who hates hippies and gays from the Left Coast and Edmund P. James, who can figure out that my bathroom window is on the left side of the sink by studying the contours of my shave? You can't. You'll think too much; become paralyzed with indecision; and start to speak in tongues. It's like what they tell criminals when they get them in the box: It's easy to tell the truth, because you only have to remember one story. But when you start to lie, you have to remember that lie, and the next lie, and the one after that, and the one after that. You have to be smart to lie. And no one's that smart. So tell the truth. Have a thick skin. Not take things personally. But, of course, when you are putting yourself out there, how could it not be personal. Unless of course you're just going to spin the records. In which case you're completely disposable. Dispensable. You might just as well be a machine.

CHAPTER FIVE

Longue Vue is this beautiful nineteenth century estate, with a giant Greek revival type mansion and these large, carefully orchestrated gardens, which were modeled after the Generalife Gardens of the Alhambra in Spain. The house, which at one time belonged to a wealthy New Orleans cotton broker, had been converted into a decorative art museum, while people have weddings and other kinds of receptions and things on the lawn. There was a trellis of jasmine and honeysuckle vines which bordered the walkway, leading up to a stairway of flowers and greens. There were a few lights on in the mansion, and there was also a good bit of moonlight coming down over the tulip beds, which were closed, and down over all the irises and white azaleas beside the lilyturf and leonara. At the edge of the gardens, where we were, was a long rectangular fountain, and then a circular fountain, which formed an i. Edmund and I were standing off to the left beside a brick wall, while Beverly stood beneath a streetlamp, watching the sidestreet and forming a visor with her hands over her eyes. A light carpet of fog was creeping in from the west, and the light was sifted over the ground.

"That was a good bit of showmanship with the cab driver" Edmund was saying.

"What's that?"

"Making your young lady friend aware of your all-too-modest fame."

"I don't think she was very impressed."

"You don't think so?"

"Nah. I think–" I started to say, when all of the sudden, this man crept up behind us and tapped Edmund on the arm. "You guys come with a Winston?"

"Yes" she said, turning, "I am Beverly Winston, and these are my friends."

"Neither of you two guys are cops, huh?" the man asked us.

"No" she promised, "they're just friends."

The man nodded his head and extended his hand for Miss Winston, and we were escorted to a limousine. It was long, and black, with tiny yellow lights that lined the windows behind the door. The driver held one of the doors open, and I was seated across from Beverly, who examined the liquor bottles of Scotch and Beefeater gin. There was a little television set that swivelled away into this little plastic cabinet, and a radio dial overhead.

The driver was wearing a St. Christopher's medallion. He was a lot like Bert Young, or Danny DeVito, or that guy that was in Miller's Crossing and used to be on Homicide. He was dressed in a grimy funeral jacket, with hairy fingers and a small facial scar. When he finally got settled, he started the engine, and we drove away through the fog.

The interstate was pretty much empty, with alternating rows of streetlamps that formed circular orange patterns on the road. There were a few other cars out, though, that evening. Some hatchbacked Toyota Supras, boxcar Cadillacs, and souped up Mustangs with their polished fenders and headlights heading off into the diamond forest of half-lit skyscraper office buildings underneath the orange and purple clouds.

"Where do you suppose we're going?" asked Beverly. I don't know, I confessed. It looked like we were going back down town.

We passed the O'Keefe Street exit, and for a second I thought we were going over the bridge. But we got off at St. Charles, taking a right at the Wendy's, passing Uglesich's, and turning left onto Baronne.

We journeyed through the rows of double-shotgun homes and old dilapidated buildings, where plywood boards were tacked across the windows and garbage was everywhere on the sidewalks and in the streets. There were a few guys with flashlights working under the hood of an old Pontiac, while groups of young men huddled on the corners with liquor or cigarettes and beer.

Finally we came to a large abandoned building at the edge of a field. It was raised on what appeared to be a giant brick slab, with weeds climbing up over the porch beneath a large wooden door. The boards had been ripped from all of the windows, with paint and plaster crumbling from every wall. "Is this where you're taking us?" asked Beverly. "Because there's no way I'm going in there."

But on the other side of the building was a European style mansion that was partially hidden behind a row of variegate bushes and among the ancient trees. There was a grassy courtyard to the right, and some slave quarters which had been converted into what appeared to be a guest house behind the yard. This must have once been in the Garden District, I was thinking, while a bronze plaque related the historical origins of the home. "Leathers House" Edmund read aloud, "erected 1859, by Captain Thomas P. Leathers, notable Mississippi River steamboatman who, during a fifty-seven year career on the river, built and commanded seven steamboats called Natchez, including the one which raced the Robert E. Lee in 1870. Here he died June 13th, 1896, at the age of eighty."

There were two oil lanterns beside the doorway, where Edmund examined the tiny Buddha knocker and the delicate hand-carved frame. I knocked on the door, which was answered by a woman with chestnut eyes and dark Egyptian skin. She looked just like Yul Brynner's wife in

The Ten Commandments, and was wearing a yellow turban, with a yellow sash, and white loose-fitting clothes.

We came inside and closed the door, and then followed the woman down an ill-lit passageway. At the end of the hall was a puzzling yellow light, and what appeared to be some kind of disinfectant or steam. The woman stopped and extended her arm towards the opening, and we found ourselves standing in the doorway of an L-shaped library.

There was a round man slouched behind a desk. He had this red hair, almost orange, which curled up in patchy little tufts above his ears and matched the tangerine bushes over his eyes so that he looked like Bozo the Clown. The man was wearing silk pajamas, with a dark paisley robe. He was writhing his hands together, and shifted from side to side in his chair. There was a humidifier in the corner, which along with a fire in the fireplace, accounted for the vapor and the steam. "Your servant, Miss Winston" he said. "Your servant, gentlemen. Please, step into my sanctum. It's a small place, I admit, but furnished to my liking. My oasis in the wasteland, among the knife-fights and the slot machines."

Beverly and I were seated in a pair of antique Chinese armchairs. Edmund stood without sitting at the edge of the couch. He was studying the romantic nineteenth century oil paintings, depicting naval battles and foggy London scenes. They each had gilded frames. The fireplace was flanked by two enormous vases, which bordered an exquisite Kurdistan rug. And on the mantlepiece was a tiny silver lamp in the shape of a dove.

"Ellsworth Frankel" the man said, still rocking from side to side. The fire was reflected in his bifocals. "And you are Miss Beverly Winston. Charming, charming. And you gentlemen are?"

"I am Edmund James, and this is my companion, Robert Wilson."

"You will excuse my anxiety" the man said. "I am plagued by a good deal of arthritis, and have long had suspicions about my heart. If your father's had been stronger, Miss Beverly, he would still be alive today."

We sat in silence, for a moment, as a tear surfaced on Beverly's cheek, and she averted her eyes to the floor. She sniffled a few times, wiping her cheeks and whispering "I knew that he was dead."

"I can give you every detail" the man said. "And what's more, I can offer you justice, regardless of whatever my brother might say. But I must have assurances that everything remains between us."

Everything stopped for a minute, and I was attempting to comfort Beverly; trying to remember what Jimmy Stewart might say, or Spencer Tracy, and forgot momentarily that Edmund and Frankel were in the room.

"For my part" Edmund was saying, "whatever you say will go no further." I then realized what was happening, and nodded in accord.

"Before we begin, then, may I offer you a glass of chianti? Mint julep? A fresh cigar?" Beverly drew another cigarette from her handbag, and placed it nervously in her mouth. "Well then" said our host, "now that we are settled. When I first decided to make myself known to you, Miss Winston, I might have given you my address, but I feared that you might have disregarded my request to refrain from contacting the police. The thing my brother fears most is attention or publicity. I myself live, as you see, wrapped in an atmosphere of elegance and art, and therefore find nothing more objectionable than a policeman or other common rogue. That landscape is a genuine Durante, and that—"

"Look" Beverly snapped. "I have come here, at your request. You send us on a paranoid goose-chase all over the city, and then bring us down into the middle of the ghetto late at night. Then you tell me my father is dead. Now, I don't mean to be rude, but I don't care what paintings you have hanging on your wall. Tell me what you have to tell me, so I can go home."

"I do apologize" the man said. "Please forgive my insensitivity. I will start at the very beginning, but I must admit that there are some facts of which I myself am ignorant. My father, as you may have guessed, was Henry Frankel. We are descended from the great Captain Leathers, of whom you have read on the doorpost, but as my great-great-grandfather, Benjamin Leathers, had only daughters, we have been disassociated from that name. In any matter, my father and your father served together in that political fiasco known commonly as the police action in Vietnam. After the war, as you know, they ventured often into South America, hunting reptiles to make purses and boots of their skin.

"I remember well when your father disappeared" he continued. "We read the details in the newspaper, and knowing that he had been a friend of our father's, we discussed the matter frequently with him. He surmised with us often, and posited hypotheses and suppositions, never giving a clue that he knew all the time what had happened to him. We did know, however, that father was always in fear of his life, and employed boxers and retired midshipmen to serve as porters at our home. On one occasion, he even fired his revolver at a man with a wooden leg, who turned out to be a Bible salesman from the plains of Arkansas. At the time, my brother and I thought this was merely an intoxicated whim of my father's, but subsequent events have lead us to change our minds.

"About fifteen years ago, my father received a letter from South America which was a great shock to him. He had suffered for years from an enlarged spleen for some time, but soon became very ill. He sent for my brother and I, so that he could tell us goodbye, and we came to see him, wrapped in a blanket, pale and shivering in his bed. He asked us to lock the door. Then, taking our hands, he told us of the secret he shared with your father, and the story of how he died.

"There is an orphan, he told us. She lives in Washington. And we owe to her a great debt. Greed is both blind and foolish, he told us. I have held on to a great treasure for years, and made nothing of it, and yet I have deprived this innocent child of her rightful succession, and I fear a great deal more. Please, my sons, give Miss Beverly Winston her father's share.

"And now I will tell you of poor Winston's death, he continued. You see, when we were in South America, we came across a great number of emeralds. The finest emeralds, it is said, in the entire world. I brought them back to America, and on the night of Winston's return, he came to collect his share. We quarreled over a proper division, and words became heated. In a fit of anger, poor Winston suffered a heart attack, and fell, striking his head down upon the corner of the desk. When I went to him, I found, to my horror, that he was dead.

"I feared that I would be charged with his murder, and an official inquiry would certainly require the existence of the treasure to be revealed. I was pondering over the matter, when I looked up and saw my servant standing in the doorway. He assured me, stepping into the room and bolting the door. Don't worry, he said, we will bury the body, and no one will ever know. I did not kill him, I said. He had a heart attack, and fell, striking his head. Come on, Mister Frankel, you don't have to lie to me. I heard you two fighting. We'll bury the body and no one will ever know.

"I realized, of course, at that point, that if I could not convince even my faithful servant of my innocence, there was no way I would be able to persuade twelve of my peers. We disposed of the body that night, and reports of Stephen's disappearance surfaced in the newspaper for several days. My days are numbered now, he said, and I ask that you boys make restitution to his child.

"It was then that he showed us the necklace, now in your possession, I trust, assuring the two of us that this was only the tip of the iceberg, as it were. It was then, presumably, when he would tell us where the emeralds were hidden. But he suddenly pointed to the bedroom window, crying no, keep him from me, my sons.

"We rushed to the window, and found nothing. But when we turned back to our father, his head had dropped to the pillow, and he was dead.

"We searched and searched for the emeralds everywhere, digging and digging, all around the grounds. Nevertheless, in the spirit of kinship, and in the hopes that someday our fathers' treasure would surface, I took it upon myself to send Miss Winston the necklace, as my father wished upon his death. My brother does not share my liberal views on such issues, but we are a family of wealth, as you can see, and I truly do not need any more. The French have a very neat way of putting these things. Le mauvais gout mene au crime.

"In any matter, a great discovery has been made. And that is why I have summoned you here. My brother has discovered the emeralds at our family plantation, a mere two hours drive from this very house. We need only go to him, and demand our rightful share."

"Where did he find them?" Edmund wondered.

"When my father first returned from South America, he traveled to the plantation house first, before coming to New Orleans. We therefore hypothesized that the treasure must have been hidden somewhere within its grounds. My brother, after digging for ten long years, discovered that while the plantation house is seventy-four feet high, the sum of all the stories, and all of the spaces between the stories, is only seventy feet, leaving four feet unaccounted for. He climbed to the top of the house, and stood in the center of our family library. He knocked the plaster from the ceiling, and sure enough, there was an extra four feet in the turret, where an iron chest was mounted across two boards. My brother lowered the chest, and there, he assures me, it remains."

"It's late" said Edmund, "and I have something at eleven tomorrow morning. So why don't we all drive out there together tomorrow night."

"How do you know that his brother won't take all the treasure for himself, and run off with it?"

"My brother does not know that I have contacted you" answered Frankel. "The bond between me and my brother is firm, I assure you. He would not even consider depriving me of my share."

"If he were" noted Edmund, "he would not have told Ellsworth of the discovery. He would have just kept his mouth shut, and taken all the gemstones for his own."

"Tomorrow evening then."

"Can you wait that long?" I asked Beverly.

"She's waited fourteen years" answered Edmund. "The sweetest nectar is that least easily attained."

CHAPTER SIX

"I feel guilty" Beverly was saying. "I never really knew my father, but still, I should feel sad that he is gone."

When my father died, I never cried at the funeral. Then, a couple of weeks later, I saw something in the paper that I knew would interest him, and I went to go call him, to tell him about it, and it wasn't until that moment, that it really hit me that he was gone.

I had asked Beverly if she wanted to grab a cup of coffee or something. There are a lot of neat coffee houses popping up among the art galleries and antique stores all down Magazine, but as Beverly was essentially a tourist, she wanted to get a few beignets.

"So what are you gonna do with your treasure?" I asked her.

"I don't know" she said. "Buy a corvette or something. Buy a yacht, and sail around the world. I love the water. We used to go to Annapolis, and just stand there for hours looking at all of the beautiful ships and the sailboats. Eat Chesapeake oysters, and crabs."

"They have blue crabs there, right?" I asked her. "Virginia's for lovers. Maryland's for crabs."

"What's that" she asked, "a bumper sticker?"

"I don't know where it's from" I told her. "I heard Katie Couric say it a couple weeks ago on tv."

"I can't watch Bryant Gumbel" she said.

Beverly was stirring her coffee. There was a sugar dish on the table, and a dish of Nutrasweet and Sweet & Low packets, and some cream. Beverly, I now knew, liked her coffee black, with the pink stuff – those things are important. My first date liked cream and sugar; she even liked cream in her tea. My best friend in college refused to use Sweet & Low because she was scared of saccharin, while my mom refuses to try Equal because she hates Raquel Welch. In any event, I was watching Beverly sip at the top of her coffee cup. Her eyes were red and watery, but her cheeks were cold and dry.

"So they have blue crabs in Maryland, right?" I asked her.

"Yeah" she said, "but they steam them. And then throw this Old Bay stuff on them, on the outside."

"It's basically the same thing as crab boil?"

"No, it's more like seasoning salt" she explained. "It tastes like Lowery's, or Tony Chacherey's."

"They're good that way?"

"Oh yeah."

I have always wanted to go to Annapolis and Baltimore, I told her. That is where they make all of those great Barry Levinson movies; Diner and Tin Men and Avalon. I love those films. People are now crediting Quentin Tarantino with bringing good dialogue back into Hollywood, and Quentin's movies are excellent, don't get me wrong. But really, it was Barry Levinson that put great dialogue back into movies. Hell, Tin Men's probably the best dialogue movie ever made. And that's all it takes. That's what New Orleans needs. One great director. And now you have a network television series and a whole slew of movies being produced in, of all places, Baltimore.

"I met my first love there" she told me. "He was really naive and romantic. He used to send me roses, and do all kinds of crazy stuff. One time he even serenaded me. But he would get drunk and go off. One night he was out drinking with all of his friends, and somebody bet him a hundred dollars to jump into the Potomac, and he drowned."

"That's a shame."

"I'm sorry" she said. "I shouldn't have said anything."

"No" I assured her. "It's okay."

Beverly was staring off into the distance. She was watching the steamboat casinos on the river and the lovers crossing the moonwalk holding hands. There was a group of people huddled about a telescope, and some old men playing chess against the wall. They sprung up right after In Search Of Bobby Fisher came out; any way for a bum to make a buck, I guess.

Most of the tables around us were empty. There were a few twentysomething couples who were eating beignets while they spoke of the latest Sienfeld episodes. The college students, on the other hand, were drinking coffee and smoking cigarettes, while they read contemporary novels and sifted through Vogue and Cosmopolitan magazines. Across Decatur Street, the wrinkled mules were still staggering around like broken horses with their empty buggies, while in the distance a man was playing the saxophone.

"So what about you?" she asked me. "You want to get your own television show?"

Nah, I told her. My father was a radio man from San Antonio. He used to tell stories. Do the news. He did talk shows, read poems, he did everything. We didn't even have a television in our house when I was growing up. Only the movies on Sunday evenings, and the radio. I love television, I told her, don't get me wrong. But I would never do television. The time is too valuable. It's too expensive. You don't have time to develop the issues. There's no spontaneity. Everything is scripted and staged.

Plus, I told her, there are no distractions in radio. You have to concentrate on the substance, because the appearances are stripped away. You know what I'm saying? It's like, who ever listens to Jane Pauley, or Susan

Roesgen, or Leeza Gibbons. You think anyone watches Kathie Lee Gifford to find out what happened to her stupid little kid? Hell no. They want to see what she's wearing, how she looks, what she's doing with her hair. Michelle Pfieffer is one of our best actresses, but because she's so pretty, nobody cares. Melanie Griffith, on the other hand, shows her tits and everybody loves her, and she couldn't even cut it in a high school play. I love television and movies, don't get me wrong. But radio is better. It's like reading. Everything is up to your imagination. It's all ideas.

"I was always an ear person" she said, lighting a cigarette. "Like when I was in school, I could read things a thousand times, and I still wouldn't remember them. But if I heard the teacher say it, just once, I would remember it forever."

"Yeah, I was the very same way."

"So you are good friends with Mister James?" she asked me.

"We're decent friends" I said. "We work in the same building, so we go to lunch every once in a while."

"He seems very intelligent."

"Oh yeah. He's very intelligent. He's a really good guy."

"It seems weird that he's a private detective."

"Yeah, well, he wanted to be a cop. He grew up with all these guys that all became cops, and he tried like hell to be a cop, and to join the FBI. He got the highest score ever on the police academy entrance exam. But he just couldn't ever pass any of the physicals. He dieted. Worked out. He tried everything, but he just couldn't do it."

"That's sad."

"Yeah, but he has a pretty good practice" I explained. Most private detectives are hired by attorneys, it seems to me. They do computer searches to find out where witnesses are, so they can serve them with papers, or find out if they have criminal records, or where else they have been sued. They take surveillance videos for the defendants, trying to catch some poor guy mowing the grass in his front yard or playing ball with his kids. Then there are the wives, of course, who cheat on their husbands, and the husbands who cheat on their wives. And Edmund does all of that. But he does police work as well. The cops or sometimes even the defense attorneys come and ask him for help every once in a while, when they get a hard case. They tease him a lot, but underneath it all, I think there is a lot of respect.

Beverly lifted her coffee cup, but it was empty. She inhaled one last time, and snubbed the cigarette in her tray. "I can't believe that my father is really dead" she then told me. "I mean, I guess I always knew it in my heart. But when you finally know, for sure, it's different."

"I could stay with you tonight" I offered, "if you're upset."

"That's okay" she said. "I'll be fine. We have a long day ahead of us tomorrow. You go ahead."

CHAPTER SEVEN

A few weeks ago, a friend of mine told me, 'You have to watch this tv show, ER, it's really good.' I said, 'Well, I'm not really into that stuff. What is it, like a show about a hospital?' 'Yeah. It's really good. It's very realistic.'

So we thought it would be fun to go down to Charity, and see how well the television show ER actually reflects what is going on in a real life emergency room. And this is what we found.

9:00 p.m. In Charity Hospital, two orderlies are mopping up blood where a twenty-four year old boy has just died from a gunshot wound to the head. On the television show ER, Doctor Benton, complaining that the lounge refrigerator is always dirty, discovers that someone has stolen his sandwich.

9:03 p.m. In Charity Hospital, two kids who were clipped in the foot in a drive-by shooting are being grilled by police officers, trying to find out who it was that shot them. After telling the police officer they don't know who it was, a woman with an INCREASE THE PEACE t-shirt joins the boys, and they laugh. On the television show ER, Doctor Mark Greene and his wife are having sex on the floor.

9:05 p.m. In Charity Hospital, a resident removes an earring lodged in a young woman's ear canal. On the television show ER, a high school wrestler who passed out in the middle of a class is wheeled into the emergency room, where Doctor Benton yells clear, and shoots him with a defibrillator. Eventually, they save him.

9:12 p.m. In Charity Hospital, the EMS team radios in a report of "scrambled eggs and ham", which is the code term for a gunshot wound to the head. An apparent suicide victim is rolled in. He is brain dead, but he is being kept alive so that his organs can be donated. Meanwhile, on the television show, Doctor Greene and his wife are lying together on the floor. She asks him if he is ready for another round, and they do it again.

9:17 p.m. In Charity Hospital, a man on a stretcher who has just suffered from an epileptic seizure is trying to convince someone that he has been robbed. Meanwhile, on television, Mookie James is late for work, again. Doctor Benton is angry with Mookie, and forces him to clean the dirty refrigerator. At home, Doctor Greene is still having sex with his wife on the floor. She straddles him, wearing a robe, and eating Chinese food with a pair of chopsticks. Back at the hospital, the wrestler, who doesn't realize that he just almost died of a heart attack, is doing push-ups on his hospital gurney because he has a big match coming up and his team is counting on him.

By ten o'clock, another gunshot victim has been dragged into Charity in an ambulance, and another has walked to the hospital on foot. Apparently trying to circumscribe the requirement that all gunshot wounds be reported to the police, the young victim tells the doctor to just put a band-aid on it, and he will be fine. On television, Doctor Greene and his wife have sex one more time, and Doctor Benton, while losing a lucrative fellowship to a presumably less-qualified female doctor, has saved two more lives.

So, that's the gripping life-like realistic number one rated prime time television show, ER. Meanwhile, we are on murder number 126 here in the Big Easy, if anyone is still counting, exceeding Washington D.C., the number two city, by 23.7 percent. In addition, we will probably have to close down Charity Hospital and other services due to a three billion dollar deficit in Medicaid funds, thanks to the out-going Governor Edwards and friends.

You will be happy to know, however, that employers are going to a comprehensive HMO system, effectively replacing all of the existing insurance companies with new insurance companies.

And speaking of insurance companies, Thursday we are going to be doing a show on what has become commonly known as tort reform. Now I have been thinking about this subject for a while, and I personally think that most of this stuff is unconstitutional. I mean, what right does the Federal Government have to regulate a state court lawsuit between two private parties?

I mean you have a patient who lives in Florida, and he goes to see a Florida doctor, in a Florida hospital, and that doctor commits malpractice, in Florida, and the patient sues that doctor in a Florida court. Now, what the hell does that have to do with interstate commerce?

And that is before you even get into separation of powers, and right to trial by jury, and due process, just compensation, and access to the courts. That's just the Federalism question.

Which was really the question that was never asked with respect to all of Clinton's health care reform. There were questions about how much it was going to cost, and who was going to pay, and what would be the bureaucracy, and would it cost more or cost less, and would doctors be able to make money, and would people have to wait in line, or get the procedures they need, or go to the doctors they choose. But no one ever asked whether the government had the power. They asked whether the government should control the system. But they never asked whether the government could control the system. Had the right to control the system.

And the same can be said of welfare, social security, and medicaid. And I'm not saying that they are bad programs.

I'm not talking about whether the legislation is good or bad, or cost-effective, or effective, or fair. Those are all policy questions. The question I am asking is a functional question. It's a constitutional question. It's a question of whether the government, our government, a constitutional government, with limited powers, has the authority to create such programs. And prior to 1937, they didn't. FDR tried to pass all of these broad programs and the Supreme Court kept knocking them down. And then FDR created two more seats, and packed the Court, and the entire meaning of the Spending Power and the Commerce Clause began to change. Into this ever-expanding catch-all that justifies just about everything, and the only time the government can't do something is when it runs up against a provision in the Bill of Rights. But the question, the first question, the real question, is whether the Government has the power to do that in the first place.

Anyway, we are gonna have two lawyers here Thursday, one from a defense firm, and one from the plaintiff's bar, and they are going to be talking about this new class action against the cigarette companies, and other issues of tort reform. And I hope you join us for that, at four. But right now, we gotta take a break. And we will be right back to take your calls, right here, on news talk and sports radio, WWL 870 AM.

CHAPTER EIGHT

"My brother went to Princeton" Frankel explained, "and he's got that protestant blue blood coursing through his veins." The sun was sinking to the west, and slanted down across the windows of the car. The swales on the side of the road were filled with rainwater. It had rained pretty hard, I remember, a few days before. The frogs and the crickets were singing really loud out on the lilies, as the watersnakes swam among the reeds. Edmund was driving the Lincoln Towncar, with Frankel navigating, and Beverly and I together in the back. There were dead animals and rubber shards from eighteen-wheeler tires scattered along the shoulder, while birds and mosses filled the trees.

"But there is a dark and cruel side to my brother also" Frankel continued. "And it is this baser instinct of which we must be wary and fear."

"Did he run for city council, I seem to remember, a long time ago?"

"Yes, he dabbled in politics" answered Frankel. "His image was quite appealing in print, if you ask me, but he could never master the art of appearing on television. He sometimes stuttered, in his thoughts, and you could detect that cold inhuman quality in his eyes."

"I don't really think that cold inhuman qualities" commented Beverly, "are generally a hindrance to becoming a politician."

"To the contrary" I said, "it's a necessity. You have to be cold and inhuman, but you have to convince people that you are warm and human on tv."

"When we were children" Frankel continued, ignoring the interruption, "we found a squirrel in the forest. It was injured. I took it, and kept it in a bird cage, and placed ointment over its wounds. We fed it water, and I broke open some pecans. That evening, I woke up in the middle of the night – I was thirsty. And when I went up to get a drink of water, I noticed that the squirrel was no longer in its cage. I looked out the window, where the dog was barking. My brother was holding his fist tightly to the leash. He flung the frightened squirrel into the pasture, where it ran. When it got a fair distance away, he let go of the leash, and watched the dog chase him down."

"That's disgusting."

"I'm afraid that's Thomas" he said.

These huge McDonald's and Exxon signs towered over the treetops. There was a roadsign for GAS FOOD LODGING and a parade of headlights was forming on the other side of the highway between the horizon and the road. "I love the color of the sun when it's like this" said Beverly, staring out the window, "everything's so red and gold."

Edmund glided into the right lane and signaled a turn, as Frankel was rubbing his eyes. "No, not here" he said when he realized that Edmund was about to get off the interstate. "The next one" he said.

"Is there anyone else at the house with your brother?" Edmund asked him. "Anyone that we should be wary of?"

"No, just our servant, Elizabeth. She has been quite faithful over the years. I think she will be quite troubled if I and my brother begin to quarrel."

"Once your brother lays his eyes upon Miss Winston" I told him, "I'm sure that he will see things our way."

Frankel's plantation house was set behind a wall of pecan and oak trees strewn with moss. There were ditches and gullies and grave-like holes surrounding the plantation, with grasses and weeds growing out of the upturned soil. The moon was rising over the fields near the greenhouse, and the wailing of the crickets and the grasshoppers grew louder on the breeze.

The house itself was supported by columns. They were evenly spaced, and fell into a series of tuscan pedestals. Among the columns stood a two-story portico, where leaded glass doors on the first floor showcased the atrium, and simple doors on the second story opened to a small iron balcony above. The turret made the structure seem off balance, drawing the weight of the building to the right. It lay opposite the small brick chimney on the left, separated by an ornate balustrade. There were four camellia bushes bordering the doorway, where I plucked a small white flower, handing it to Beverly. For luck, I said.

The light from the chandelier splintered through the leaded glass onto the porch, where Frankel was ringing the doorbell. A woman was crying inside.

"Miss Alhandre! Open the door, Miss Alhandre!" Frankel was pounding on the doorframe. "It's me, Ellsworth! Open the door!"

A tiny woman came into the doorway. Her face was red, and her hair was wet and uncombed. "Mister Ellsworth, thank god you're here. Your brother has shut himself into the study" she said taking his hand. "I cannot get him to come down."

We were rushed up a great cathedral stairway, with a crystal chandelier over the landing, and a deep imperial rug. Upstairs, and down the hallway, it became darker, and we came finally to a locked door. "Thomas! Thomas, it's me!" Ellsworth was pounding. "Please Thomas, open the door."

Edmund was kneeling beneath him. He opened his pocket-knife and began to tinker with the lock. "Mister

Frankel!" Me and Beverly also were shouting. "Open the door! Open the door! Open the door!"

At that point, Edmund turned the lock, and Ellsworth tumbled through the doorway and onto the floor. The room was square. It was a study filled with shelves of books and early century magazines. In the center of the room was a desk with a reading lamp and leather chair. Seated at the desk was a large man, who was dead.

"Thomas!" Ellsworth jumped at him, but Edmund grabbed his arm. "We don't want to disturb anything" Edmund told him. "I am sorry, Ellsworth. Your brother, I presume."

"Yes, that is poor Thomas" he sniffled, "and I fear that our treasure, with him, is now gone."

CHAPTER NINE

There was a ladder behind the desk, which lead to a hole in the ceiling. There were pieces of plaster on the floor. Edmund went to the window, which was locked, and then kneeled down to examine the floor. "There were two men in this room" he then said. "One has a clubbed or wooden leg. See. It's round." And he pointed to a round mark beside a footprint in the rug. Edmund then ascended the ladder. The turret was for the most part empty, except for a few roaches and rat-droppings beside the hole in the floor. The outer wall of the turret formed a cloverleaf beside the rafters, with a two-foot (or smaller) opening. Edmund scaled down the ladder, while Ellsworth was sobbing in the doorway, and Beverly used a handkerchief to dry his cheeks and eyes.

Thomas Frankel was purple, and stiff. Blood covered his robe, and had dried around the bullet hole in his head. On the desk was piece of parchment. There was a swastika in the center, and written in blood across the bottom was THE SIGN OF FOUR.

"Go call the police" Edmund said, as I turned to the doorway. "Ellsworth" Edmund snapped. "It's not going to do you any good to remain in here. Go call the police. Tell them to come immediately. Tell them that your brother is dead."

Beverly supported his weight with her body, saying I will take him, and leading him quietly from the room.

"I think our friend is in trouble" Edmund then told me.

"Why?"

"He was here last night."

"How do you know that?"

"See those glasses on the table?"

"Yeah."

"Those are the same spectacles he was wearing yesterday evening, when we saw Frankel at his home."

"Maybe he was wearing them when we came in, and then took them off so that he could wipe his eyes."

"No."

"Do you think he did it?"

"No. If he were going to kill his brother and take the money, he would never have contacted us."

"Why not? We saw him last night in New Orleans. These back-parish coroners out here won't be able to pin down the time of death with any degree of accuracy. He'll get the maid to lie for him, and we are a perfect alibi."

"No" Edmund assured me. "He would not have us snooping around for the emeralds, if in fact there are any emeralds. The last thing you want to do if you are going to kill someone is to advertise your motive to a bunch of strangers that you're not even sure you can trust."

"But you don't have to prove motive, you just–"

"According to the law, you don't have to prove motive. But no prosecutor has ever secured a conviction without telling the jury why. Besides" he said, "Ellsworth is too small to fit through the opening."

"In the ceiling?"

"In the turret" Edmund explained. "The opening is less than two and a half feet wide, with no room to spare."

"That's how you think the murderer got in?"

"I'm pretty sure. Someone climbed in through the roof. Someone small, like a child. He tied a rope, unlocked the window, and threw it over the edge. See, here, you can see the shavings from the rope. Here are some more on the floor. This allowed the one-legged man to pull himself up to the window – I mean there is almost no way that he could have shimmied the drainpipe, or climbed a trellis with a wooden leg. And the door was locked from the inside. Right? They lowered the chest or whatever down from the window. And then the crippled man repelled his way down. The child pulled up the rope, locked the window behind him, and climbed back out through the turret, and back down the side of the wall. Then they carried off the stuff, and they were gone."

"That explains everything" I admitted, "but it just seems so overly complicated."

"A great detective once said," said the detective, "that once you have eliminated the impossible, whatever remains, however implausible, must be the truth."

"Well, well, what do we have here?" the sheriff was saying. He was a tall bulky man who looked like Rod Stieger in The Heat Of The Night with black and silver hair and handsome eyes. He had a forty-four revolver in his holster and a brass star stapled to his chest. Beverly, meanwhile, was still attempting to comfort Ellsworth, while Miss Alhandre was fixing sandwiches and making tea. There was a small man in a black suit with a camera who was taking pictures, and another law enforcement officer who was standing at the sheriff's side.

"Hello" said Edmund, extending his hand, "I am a private detective from New Orleans. This is my friend, Robert Wilson, and I am Edmund P. James."

"You Robert Wilson the radio guy?"

"Yeah."

"Well what the hell you doin up here with this fat son of a bitch and this here guy?"

"We're friends" I said. "We work in the same building."

"You found him like this?"

"Yes, officer" Edmund said. "The window was locked, and the door was locked from the inside. I think your guy must have escaped through the roof, and shimmied down the trellis or the drain."

The sheriff climbed up the ladder to the inside of the turret. "It aint but a one or two foot opening" he said. "You can't fit through that and get away."

"We think it might have been a kid" I offered.

"This aint New Orleans, Mister Wilson, with all due respect. We aint got kids sellin crack and shootin each other in the streets from the time they can crawl."

"Excuse me" said Edmund, to the man in the suit who was taking pictures, "you might wanna be careful. There are some pretty distinct footprints on the floor."

"Thanks" the man said, stepping away from the rug.

"You still haven't told us what y'all doin up here."

"Mister Frankel was worried about his brother. He retained me to come here and check on him. Robert and his friend Miss Winston decided to come along for the ride. When we got here, the housekeeper was crying. She said that Thomas here had locked himself in his room, and wouldn't come out. I picked the lock, and when we opened the door, he was dead."

"No one here but the maid then?"

"And whoever it was that shot poor Frankel here in the head."

"Did you move the body, open anything, touch anything?"

"No. Nothing beyond just climbing up the ladder and looking around where the killer made his escape."

"Why was the loser in the other room a-scared for his brother?"

"There were threats mailed to both of the two brothers on similar parchment. They thought it was a group of unsavories trying to extort money from them. That is the parchment there on the desk."

"These guys some kinda Nazis or something?"

"Not that we know of."

"The sign of four. What the hell is that?"

"Your guess is as good as ours" I said.

"Y'all go downstairs now" the sheriff told us. "I gotta talk to your client alone."

CHAPTER TEN

"And what is your name?"

"Elizabeth Alhandre."

"And what do you do?"

"I take care of Mr. Thomas, and the grounds."

I had wandered down into the kitchen and was stirring some sugar into a cup of tea when the sheriff came down and started to interview Miss Alhandre. She was an elderly woman, with gray strands blended among her brown and yellow curls. She spoke with a Spanish accent, and appeared to be tired and drained.

"Where are you from, Colombia?"

"Bolivia" she said.

That's where Butch Cassidy and the Sundance Kid went after they jumped into the gorge, to rob banks with Katherine Ross, before they died. I used to love Katherine Ross. She's beautiful. I heard she didn't like acting much. She did just those couple of movies, and then disappeared.

"And how long have you worked here?" the sheriff was asking.

"For many years" the woman said. "I used to work for Mister Frankel, the late Mister Frankel. When he died, I continued to take care of his boys."

"You were here in the house last night when Mister Frankel died?"

"Yes, I have been in the house since yesterday. But I didn't know that he was dead. I thought he was just sleeping late, and then in the afternoon, I assumed he had got up and gone for his walk. But then, at dinnertime, he never came down, and when I went upstairs he was locked behind the door."

"Anyone else been here, that you know of?"

"No" she said, "just Mister Frankel."

"The dead guy?"

"Mister Thomas" she said, "and Mister Ellsworth too."

"The brother?"

"Yes, sir."

"When was he here?"

"It was late last night. He came to see what Mister Thomas had found in the attic. They had tea together, and then he left."

"Did you see him leave?"

"No, I was in my room."

"So, Thomas could have been dead already when – what's this guy's name, Ellsworth? What the hell kind of a name is Ellsworth? When he left?"

"I suppose so" said the woman. "But Ellsworth would have never harmed his brother. If anything, it would have been the other way around."

"You mentioned something about something they found in the attic. What was that?"

"I can't tell you, sir. I don't know."

"Thank you, ma'am. We are gonna need to take you down to the stationhouse. Frankel!" he then called. "Frankel, you're gonna have to come with us, fella. We placin you under arrest."

"Oh my God."

"What's your theory there sheriff, may I ask?" inquired Edmund.

"What?"

"What's your theory of the case?"

"He come to see his brother in the middle of the night. They fought over something the brother found in the attic, probably somethin belonged to their daddy or grandaddy or somethin. This guy whacks him in the head, leaves some phony bullshit message, locks the door behind him, and dumps the key in the swamp, along with the gun. She seen him here last night, and unless she killed the poor bastard, ruby red here was just about the only one. Put the cuffs on em."

"Unhand me, you cretin."

"Shut up, tubby. I don't need no trouble outta you."

"I am innocent, unhand me" Mister Frankel again demanded, as Edmund placed his hand on the Ellsworth's shoulder. "Just relax" he said. "It is very important that you remain patient, and that you do not say anything to the police until your attorney arrives."

"You have the right to remain silent" the deputy recited, "you have the right to an attorney."

"Don't say anything to the police" Edmund again advised him, "until an attorney gets there."

"I would never entrust my welfare to one of those unsightly parasites" muttered Ellsworth, whose hands were writhing in the handcuffs while he huffed and puffed and groaned.

"Robert, why don't you take Miss Winston home" Edmund suggested. "Then I want you to go to 1023 Magnolia Street, and ask for Toby."

"Toby?"

"When you find him, bring him back here."

"Now?"

"Yes. Tonight. Immediately. I will wait for you here."

"You watch yourself, fella" the sheriff warned him. "We got a crime scene here. I don't want you messin up any prints or blood stains or anything."

"Where the hell is the coroner, doc?" asked the man with camera.

"Damned if I know" said the sheriff. "You stay here and keep an eye on this here so-called detective. I'm gonna take porky and the spick down to the jail. See what we can beat out of em – just kiddin, of course. Mister Wilson, been a pleasure. Ma'am. You sure are a sight. Let me know if you plan on gettin back up here this a-ways. I'll see to it that you are properly protected. Come on, porks, lets go."

CHAPTER ELEVEN

"Hey Bustah! Where ya at, dawlin?"

"I'm right here, my heart. Come on in here, my love, let me get a hug from ya. That's nice. All-rightie, good evenin, my hearts, and welcome back to Cookin With Ambrosia. We listenin to a little B.J. Thomas here. Thank you Mister Frost. And we doin it today, and every Tuesday. Next week we gonna be talkin about how to make your homemade ice cream, chocolate, vanilla, lemon ice, an all that...."

Beverly and I were on our way back to New Orleans in the Lincoln Towncar, with bugs slapping occasionally into the windshield and the light from the headlights creeping through the grasses and the bushes and the reeds. We were following a train of headlights which circled off into the distance towards the east and beneath the surface of the road.

"Is this your station?" she asked me.

"Uh-huh."

"You can hear it all the way out here?"

"You can hear it in Canada on a clear night" I told her. "We got fifty thousand watts pumping out all over the galaxy."

"It's weird when you think about alien life forms" she said, "from centuries away, listening to our radio and television programs with their satellites and things." I started to think about the little creatures at the end of Close

Encounters, with superintelligent faces, and long fingers, and large eyes. It's hard to imagine that evolution progresses along the same lines everywhere, I was thinking, when Beverly said, "they would be a lot like you, I think."

"What do you mean by that?"

"I get the feeling that your reality comes from radio and television."

"Where does your reality come from?" I asked.

"I don't know."

She was looking out into the darkness.

"What is reality?" she said.

I was watching the moon and the stars outside the window. The way they form a circle down from the sky. And then there is nothing. And then there is moonlight on branches. It was like a scene lifted from some Ron Howard or Steven Spielberg movie. And I was thinking about reality, and ideas.

Plato believed that nothing physical exists in reality. You can look at a car, for example, and say that it's blue. But when you look at it more closely, you see that there are really shades of grays and reds and purples. The paint is chipped and cracked, and the metal is beginning to rust. So it's not really blue, it's almost blue. Imperfect blue. And in that process, you actually deny it's blueness by comparing it to something which is blue, unconditionally blue, and so you must already know what blue is. Even though no visible thing, neither sea nor sky nor the enamel paint on our cars, is absolutely blue, then it must truly exist as an idea.

"I don't know what the hell you're talking about" she said.

"It's like, if I read a word that is written" I continued, "I can recognize it instantly because I already know the word and what it means. But if it's in a foreign language, on the other hand, then I don't see the word as it is, but only as a group of letters. I may understand the letters, but I have to read them one by one to see what the word is, and then I still probably won't know what it means. And if I don't even recognize the characters, then the writing becomes completely meaningless. It's kind of a chicken and the egg kind of a thing. Because if I not only don't know what I'm reading, but also don't know what reading is, then I can't see a book, because I don't have an idea of one."

"Nope" she said, "still doesn't help me. Sounds like a bunch of crap thought up by someone with too much time on their hands."

We turned off of the interstate and onto a highway that was flanked with Exxon stations and Texacos, with motels and hotels, with McDonald's, Time Savers, Rally's, Bud's Broilers, Popeyes, and Circle K's. The highway was lined with streetlamps, where pebbles and oyster shells filled the shoulders, and vagrants congregated with wine bottles and dirty blankets on the neutral grounds.

I've never seen a dead person before, I was thinking. I kinda think that maybe it should have upset me more than it actually did. But I really didn't feel anything.

"My grandfather worked in a mortuary" she told me.

"Really?"

"Yeah. That's how he paid his way through college."

"That's interesting" I said. It wasn't really interesting, but I said that it was. I guess it could be interesting. But you would have to know more. That's the thing about people. They want to tell you what they want to tell you, not what you want to hear.

The trick is to pretend that you are not interested in what they are saying, Edmund once told me. If you let people think that their information is important to you, they will clam up like an oyster. If you listen to them under protest, you are likely to get what you want.

Which kinda translates into radio, also, because people are generally interested in things that they know they're not really supposed to be interested in. It's kind of like the forbidden fruit. Which is really why people like Joe Pyne, Alan Berg, and Howard Stern have gotten to be so popular, and, in many ways, paved the way for the rest of us. And it's not even really the sex jokes or fart jokes or lesbians; the FCC fines and the seven dirty words that you can't – or couldn't – say on tv. It's more about what radio is, and what it's supposed to be. It's not supposed to be about four friends sitting around in a room and talking about whatever comes to mind, like it was a card game. Dissecting everything from tipping the parking attendant to Spike Lee's bullshit to Kathie Lee's clitoris to digital versus analog to whether cybersex is cheating to Batman comics and Star Trek conventions to the hypocrisy and banality, ineptitude and pomposity, of every other disc-jockey, Hollywood actress, talk show pundit, politician, or television personality. But that's what they made it, and that's why people listen.

"So who does Edmund think took the jewels?" Beverly then asked me.

"Well, the guy apparently had one leg. And it looks like he had a kid with him."

"A kid?"

"Someone who could fit in the crawl space in the roof."

"Someone short" she said to herself, "and a one-legged man."

"That's what it looks like" I said.

And she was sitting there for a minute, looking out the window, thinking. Like maybe she had someone in mind.

And I started to ask her if that sounded familiar, but, for some reason, left it alone. "Do you think that Frankel killed his brother?" she then asked me. "Nah" I told her. "Doesn't have it in him. Can you imagine that guy firing a gun? At someone else's head?"

"No" she admitted. "But looks can be deceiving."

"I mentioned that some of the dishes had a little winy taste to it" Ambrosia was saying, "wine this, and wine that. And when you get out on a live broadcast like that, you really pushin for time. So we really didn't get into, no pun intended, the meat an potatoes of the question. An we really didn't get into the actual usage, what for what, and this for that. So I been gettin a lotta mail, askin about it. Can you burn it? Will it burn? Will it ruin this, or ruin that, an all that. So we gonna do some show about wines, got some recipes, and I'm gonna tell ya, hearts, you like vidalia onions, we got a recipe here...."

"Have you ever had a vidalia onion?" I asked her.

"Yeah, they're sweet" she said. "But have you ever had a Maui onion?"

"Unh-uh."

"They're even sweeter."

"They grow them in Hawaii?"

"Yeah, they're really expensive" she said. "Even if you buy them in Maui."

"I've never been to Hawaii."

"It's beautiful" she said. "I was a swimmer in high school. And the coach promised that if we won the state championship, he would take us to Hawaii over the summer break. No one really believed him, and he never thought in a million years that we could actually win the state championship, but we did. And this one girl on the team, she stunk, but her father was really rich. I mean out of bounds wealthy. And so he sprung for the trip."

"For all of you?"

"Yeah, it was pretty cool."

"Yeah."

"It was a lot of fun."

"So you're a pretty good swimmer then?"

"State champion" she said. "Four hundred butterfly, 1981 and 1982."

"Congratulations."

"Thank you" she said. "Those were great times."

"They were okay."

"So how did you get started in radio?"

When I was really young we used to make these 8-track recordings. Me and my best friend would pretend like you were taking a trip to different parts of the country, talking about all of the sites and telling silly jokes. Then, in high school, we would practice with albums, trying to time all of the spaces between songs. It's mostly just memorizing how they begin. Like Stairway To Heaven has four rounds before the singing starts, while Sympathy For The Devil has ten. I would go to the station with my dad on weekends, and play with the equipment. He got me a job cleaning up and filing away tapes when I was sixteen, and people would show me how everything worked and what was going on. When I was by myself I would sit around with a stop watch, looking out the window. I would give myself forty seconds to describe something, and we'll be right back, or see you tomorrow, or enjoy the drive home, with Bobby Wilson, on such and such station, your all-entertainment radio network, such and such FM. Then in college I had my own show on the college station, and when I graduated someone offered me a job.

"It's a tough life" she said.

"Why, what do you do?"

"I work for a restaurant and hotel supply company. We make sure everybody's got their little packages of soap and shampoo that say Hilton, and we make sure that all the restaurants have their Lum's or Maggie's condiments, and rolls and rolls of toilet paper, and towels."

"You get stuff in bulk at a discount?"

"Yeah, that's the one perk to the job" she said. "Pistachios."

"Pistachios?"

"Yeah, I love pistachio nuts. Not the red ones. Just the plain ones, with salt. And they have these like after World War III survival size bags of pistachios."

"Are red pistachios really red?"

"No, that's not real. That's just a bunch of dye. Gets all over your hands. Probably causes cancer, like those red M&Ms."

"Red Dye Number Five?"

"Was that what it was called? Yeah. Right. Red Dye Number Five."

"Hey, J.R. here," he was saying over the radio, "talking about my good friend Bill Roohi and Abita Spring Water. Bill's kinda like the godfather of bottled water. Been thirty years in the business. He's the one that put Brand X together, built it from the ground up. And when the opportunity arose, to do things his own way..."

"Do you do these ads?" she asked me.

"I do some spots, but I do them live, as part of the show. These are recorded."

"Is free spring water your job perk?"

"No, not spring water. I get Zima, and free Blockbuster rentals, and meals at Russell's Marina, and City Business magazine."

"Is that on the books or off."

"A little of both" I said. "But seriously, J.R. has a great deal, because he gets paid extra, by the spot. So he can make an extra twenty or thirty thousand a year just on that. I do them as part of my contract."

"So you have to do so many, for so many of the station's sponsors, per month or per year?"

"Yeah, basically. That's why Howard Stern has such a bad deal, or at least had a bad deal – I'm sure he has negotiated a new contract by now. But he does tons of spots. And didn't get paid extra for any of them. They were in his contract. And he is doing these local spots for Joe's Bike Shop, and Jalapenos, and Fred's Water Beds, and stuff, as part of his contract, when he could have been making a fortune just concentrating on the big things, like Yahoo, and ETV."

"Do you feel like you are just prostituting yourself for these products?"

"Not really" I said. "I don't personally do spots for any product that I wouldn't vouch for. I will run spots on anything, but I won't personally record them. So it's not so bad. Plus the fact that they give me the forum to speak to thousands of people, about whatever I want, every day. You do what you gotta do. And that's the way it is."

After I dropped Beverly off at the hotel, I drove over to Magnolia street, where it was pretty quiet and dark. When I dropped her off, Beverly put her hand on my thigh. She said goodnight, Robert, thank you, and leaned over to give me a kiss. Her lips were soft, and warm, and I had been thinking about them the rest of the night.

I moved quietly up the wooden steps to the porch of a Queen Anne cottage with 1023 posted in brass over the door. The weatherboards and porch banisters were dirty and partly rotted, with scales of paint broken and torn. The house was dark, except for the porchlight, and all of the sudden, what sounded like a thousand dogs started barking and howling as soon as my fingers touched the door.

"God damn, son of a bitch!"

I ran down off the porch and stood at the bottom of the steps, calling Toby. A light went on in the hallway, and the figure of a man was struggling through the window behind the door. "Shut up!"

"Toby?" I was calling. "Toby?" "Mister Toby?"

"Shut up, you damn dogs" the man said, and then asked me what the hell I wanted from behind the door. "Is Toby there?"

"Who wants to know?"

"My name is Robert Wilson. I am looking for a guy named Toby."

"Who sent you?"

"Edmund James."

"Okay, I'm a comin" he said.

The man opened the door and six or seven dogs came at me like a pack of wolves. "Don't pay em no mind" the man told me, and sure enough they were licking at my hands and rubbing against my thigh. I looked up at the man, who was scratching his ear, and motioned me to come inside. He was tall and thin, with a long white beard that fell from just beneath his eyes. His skin was worn and dirty, with yellow nails, and an old terrycloth robe. "Eddie sent you to me?"

"Yes, sir. Robert Wilson. Pleased to meet you. Sorry it's so late."

"It's one in the mornin, son."

"I know" I said. "I apologize."

"Well come on in" the man said turning, and motioned me again with his hands. I stepped through the doorway. "Don't touch anything" he said.

There were cages of parrots and cockatoos, with dogs and cats and rabbits lining the walls. The six or seven dogs that hadn't been chained or caged up followed us through the house, licking at my hands and barking incessantly. There were fish tank aquariums, and bamboo cages filled with Vietnamese pot-belly pigs. "I'll sell you one cheap" the man told me. "What?" I asked. "The pig?"

"Yeah" the man said. "They big."

"How much you sell them for?"

"I could go–" "Holy shit!" I jumped halfway out of my ass, and came down staring at the mouth of a tremendous boa constrictor snake. "That's just Charlene" the man told me. "I let her loose to keep out the roaches and the mice."

The kitchen was small and cold, with a broken white refrigerator and a dirty sink. There was a newspaper lying on the breakfast table, (a small table), and a coffee pot resting on the stove. The man opened up a screen door in back, where more dogs from outside began to bark. "Toby" he called. "Get your ass over here Toby. Mister Eddie got somethin for you. You be a good dog, now, with this here fella. Come on."

"This is Toby?" I asked.

"The one and only" the man said. "The best damn blood hound from here to West Virginia." The man handed me a leash and offered me a cup of coffee. But it was getting pretty late, and I still had to drive back out to meet

Edmund. At this rate, I wasn't getting home until about five. So I said that's okay, no thank you, and we were gone.

CHAPTER TWELVE

"The child stepped in creosote" Edmund was explaining. "It must have been on the roof to treat the wood, mixed in with the tar." The detective was standing with a flashlight at the east end of the house, beside the drain. He showed me five or six bullets, which he had found on the ground there, but they were free of fingerprints, he said. Toby, the dog, was soaking up the scent from an oily footprint, and led us away through the trees.

"They must have escaped in a boat down the river" the detective surmised. "That is why Miss Alhandre never heard a car."

At the bank of the river was a wooden boat-launch. Edmund knelt down and examined the fresh footprints beside the pier in the mud. To the north were reeds and grasses on the levee, where the hum of crickets and frogs was almost deafening. To the south was a shantytown of cabins. It looked like something right out of Tom Sawyer or Huckleberry Finn. There were a few horses and some machinery near a fence, and a fire, and a plow.

"Probably the slave quarters a hundred and fifty years ago" Edmund was saying.

"And here they are today."

We made our way with Toby over to the cabins where an old man wearing overalls was carving a face into the side of a walking-stick, while an elderly woman was knitting beside the fire.

"What y'all want so late in the evenin?" asked the woman.

"A man was killed up at the house last night."

"Well we don't know nothin about it."

"What's goin on, grams?" a child poked his head out from inside the cabin. The child was barefoot, with a black t-shirt and blue jeans that were soiled.

"You go on back to bed."

"Were you out here last night?" asked the detective.

"I was sleepin" the child said.

"You sure you didn't see anything? Anything at all."

"Sibyl seen something" the old man said.

"Don't you tell them nothin, Albert."

"They're okay, I suspect" the man said. "Sibyl seen somethin last night. But she gone."

"Where did she go?"

"Off to Franklin. She got kin there."

"Did she tell you what she saw?"

"Yesterday evenin we seen a boat at the launch. Little boat for this river. Black with yellow trim. On the back it say The Cherokee Queen. No one knew who it belonged to, but in the middle of the night, Sibyl heard a scuffle. She went down there a bit yonder, and seen a man with a wooden leg. She say he was carryin a chest with this – whaddaya call em? Little people. And they climbed into the boat and sailed on."

CHAPTER THIRTEEN

Ellsworth Frankel was rocking nervously in his chair at the long end of the table, with cold flourescent lights vibrating over his head. The deputy was seated across from him. He had a tape recorder and a notepad on the table, and a standard WAIVER OF MIRANDA RIGHTS form. The room was damp and cold, with broken plaster walls and cement floors.

"If you're telling the truth" the deputy was saying, "I suggest taking the test, and it's gonna show up. And if you're not telling the truth, if you did that, you know, yourself, then we need to talk about it and try to get it straightened out. For whatever reason. If it was money, you're a human being. Everybody makes mistakes. Including myself. I've done things wrong. So, it's like I say, you being a human being and everything, you're subject to making mistakes; but when you make a mistake, you know, how do you get over that mistake? Because you have to get over it. You have to admit that you made a mistake, ask for forgiveness from the Lord, or whatever, and then you can get it straightened out. Okay? Hey, look, you're not the first person that made a mistake, flew off the handle, or whatever. We all make mistakes. And if he held something over your head, you need to tell me about it. I don't think you're a bad person. I don't think you're a bad guy. It's not like you killed seven or eight people or whatever. It was a spur of the moment, a one-time deal. We know that. Maybe he was stealing from you, maybe he was blackmailing you, I don't know. But it happened, and it's over with, and now it's just a matter of time."

Edmund had asked me to go to the sheriff's office to check on Mister Frankel. I asked the sheriff if I could observe the interrogation. The deputy protested, but the sheriff was a fan of the show. They seemed happy about the fact that Frankel had not asked for an attorney, and I think the sheriff thought that I would be a perfect witness if anyone were to allege that the confession had been coerced. From my point of view, I was curious, and I knew that they wouldn't get too rough with Frankel as long as I was there. From everything I hear, it's not like the old days; they don't really beat confessions out of people anymore. But then, you never know.

"Because all of these things come out into the open" the deputy was explaining. "It's very rare that something like this doesn't get solved. I'm just giving you the chance to get it off your chest, and we can clear the whole thing up right now. And then things will go easy on you. Because if you go to the judge, and you say, 'Look, I did it, but I'm sorry, and this is the reason why I did it,' then he is gonna listen to that. He is gonna listen to you. They're human beings. They're not bad guys. I don't think you're a bad guy, but if you did it, and you keep saying, 'I didn't do it, it wasn't me,' then they are gonna treat you like a son of a bitch, and make damn sure you never see the light of sunshine again."

The deputy was tall and lean with red hair. He wore a pair of reading glasses over his eyes. His uniform was well-ironed, and he had both a watch and a ring. I was mostly concentrating on Frankel, though. His hands were cuffed together, and his wrists had started to turn pretty red. His feet were unshackled, however, and tapped anxiously on the floor. The sound from the light fixtures grew louder, and beads of sweat had formed on Ellsworth's bald-spot over his brow. He squirmed in his chair, rubbing his damp cheeks. It was just like NYPD Blue, or Law & Order, or Homicide.

"How old are you, Mister Frankel?"

"Forty-one."

"Forty-one. I'm thirty myself" the deputy said. "It's scary when you think about it really. Cuz you never know when you're gonna go. You never know when the good Lord is gonna call your number. You know? He might come right now. And so I always try to have my life straightened out, at all times, cuz we really never know. This building could fall down and I'd be gone. The same with you. You might be riding home tomorrow, and have this hanging on your shoulders, that you did this, and you don't want to go that way, I don't think, you don't want to go out that way, because eternity is a long, long time. I don't know if you believe in God, Mister Frankel. I don't know if you believe in the Devil, or the afterlife. I know I do. And I sure as hell wouldn't want to go out with something like this hangin over my head, because that is just where we'd be goin. So I'm just gonna ask you one question. What would you do if you were God? Or Saint Peter? Standin at the gates. What would you do if you were the judge? Wouldn't you go easier on someone who's been straight up? Wouldn't you go easier on someone that came in and said, 'Well, judge, I made a mistake. This is what happened. This is why it happened. But I'm sorry.' And then explain how he had a good reason and all for what happened, like maybe it was an accident, or blackmail, or self-defense or something, and those guys get out okay. I'm not gonna lie to you and tell you that you're not gonna go to prison or anything, but at least you won't go there for a lifetime, which is a long, long time. And there's a difference. There sure as hell is a difference. And so it's just basically a matter of which way you wanna go on the deal. Do you wanna talk about what happened?"

"I do" replied Ellsworth. The deputy handed him the waiver of rights form, where Frankel signed his name at the bottom and initialed every line.

"They have a newspaper article about your friend Frankel" the program manager was saying. He tugged at his moustache, and flipped to the Metro section, where a study will explore the impact of the New Orleans gaming industry.

"You're not listening to me" I told him. "This woman is so beautiful. She's... majestic. That's the best word that I can use to describe her. She – the way she moves. It's like she glides. You know? She moves like a ballet dancer. Or an ice skater. Skating along from side to side. It's so... sexual."

"Did you fuck her?"

"Don't say that" I told him. "It's disrespectful."

"She's a redhead?"

"Yeah."

"That's good."

"What do you mean?"

"I mean that's good" he said. "Good" he said, "as opposed to bad."

"She's got red hair, but it's not flaming red. It's a deep dark red. Almost brown. And these beautiful green eyes. And she's very different looking. Very unusual, but attractive. Cold and distant, in a way, but sexy."

"Sounds good."

He tugged again at his moustache, looking to the Living section, with HOT-headed heroes and COLD-blooded villains, heart WARMing love stories & treats for the KOOL-Aid crowd.

My producer, Allison, was back from her camping trip. She was handing the guest a cup of coffee and keeping him entertained. Allison was a typical girl from Long Island, with tangled black hair, and brown eyes, and dark skin.

They come down in their BMWs and their Saabs to go to Tulane, they like it, and they stay.

But Allison was a really good person. She was a big girl, with big hips and big boobs, and a very warm smile. She was wearing a sexy black dress on her body, and a pair of white basketball high-tops on her feet. That was another advantage of radio. It doesn't really matter what you wear.

"It's good to see you again" I said to the guest. "I really enjoyed your book." He thanked me, and sipped from the coffee mug while I ushered him into the booth. He sat in the chair to my left near the window, placing his coffee to his right and adjusting his microphone. There were seven seconds left on the trailer, six, five, four, three, two, one.

"Good evening, I'm Bobby Wilson, and we are here today with Steven Rendall, senior analyst with FAIR, Fairness and Accuracy in Reporting, and one of the authors of The Way Things Aren't, Rush Limbaugh's Reign of Error, which goes into depth concerning, what, specifically, Mister Rendall?"

"It's a compilation, it's non-exhaustive, and it only accounts for things that have been said during the last ten months, but it's the one hundred and thirty most illustrative, or in our opinion, the most egregious lies, that have been told by Rush Limbaugh over the past ten months."

"Such as?" I said. "Give us a few examples."

"Well, he said that the New York Times, prior to the November 8th election, had not done one story on the Republican's Contract with America; when, in fact, the New York Times had published more than one article a day for the last 40 days, a total of 45 articles, regarding the Contract With America by the day of the election. He said that there are more acres of forest land in America today than there were when Columbus discovered the continent. While the truth is that in 1492, there was over a billion acres of forest land in the United States, while today there is only seven hundred and thirty-one million. In a similar statement, he said that there are more Native Americans living in the United States today than there were when Columbus came over, when, in fact, there are only around three million Native Americans on the continent today, while there were over ten million Native Americans living here in 1492. These are facts. They're not liberal facts or conservative facts, those are just facts. They're misstatements. They're falsehoods. Which he uses to advance his political agenda."

"But let me just say, Steven, that his books, his radio show, three hours a day, and his tv show, five days a week, that's a lot of time. Anybody doing that much is bound to be inaccurate, especially when much of it is live, off the cuff. I mean I'm sitting here talking with you, and there's absolutely no script. We fly by the seat of our pants. And Rush Limbaugh will tell you, he's on the air primarily for entertainment. He's a radio talk show host. He's not a journalist. There's a different standard."

"Well, first of all, it's not just what he is saying on his radio show. It's things that he says in his books, in his newsletter, and on his television show, which are scripted. They're not impromptu. And second of all, actually, Rush is now beginning to call himself a journalist. He did it on David Brinkley last week, and he's referred to himself as a journalist several times quite recently."

"Well let me just say, before we go to a few callers, that the standard on this show is information. We let people give their opinions all day long, but when the caller starts reporting facts, and I have no way of determining whether those facts are true, or whether that information is accurate, that's where I draw the line. And that is really what you're concerned about, correct?"

"Yeah. Exactly. Rush Limbaugh or anyone else can get up there all day long and give their opinion about why Democrats are better than Republicans, or why this candidate is better than that candidate, or this plan is better than that plan. But Rush is passing on information to his callers, factual information, which he is reporting as if it's the truth. And a lot of the time, it isn't."

"Leo, you're on the air, with Steven Rendall."

"Got one question for you, Steve."

"Sure."

"I don't know why you're writing a book against Rush" he said. "If you want to write a book, you should write a book about Bill Clinton, the biggest liar in the history of mankind. I would buy that."

"Well first let me say that we are a media watch group. And Limbaugh is a media phenomenon. As are ABC, NBC, Nightline, MacNeil Lerher, and all the other groups that we have done reports on. But the purpose of our group is to scrutinize journalists, not politicians. So we would never do a piece on Bill Clinton, just like we would never do a piece on Ronald Reagan, or Newt Gingrich, or Bob Dole. I would also like to point out that FAIR has called, during periods where Clinton was getting pretty puff treatment by the media, we have called for much stronger harder coverage of Clinton, and especially following the money. Indeed, we are on the record as calling for the media to spend more time looking into Whitewater, especially before the 1992 election, when it could have made a difference. We continue to think that there is an issue of money, and an issue of a conflict of interest there. So if you're curious, call the Whitehouse, and they will tell you that we are no friend of the Clintons."

"Tom, you're on WWL."

"Hello Bobby, and mega dittos to you, Mister Rendall."

"Thanks."

"Contrary to what Honest Abe Lincoln postulated, apparently you can fool all of the people all of the time, as long as you reflect their political ideology in an entertaining way. This is my question to you: By and large, Rush gets a sweetheart press; why hasn't more of the, quote, mainstream liberal press, unquote, tried to sharpshoot Rush's piffy persiflage?"

"I think a lot of the print press, where every mainstream paper has a beat reporter who covers television, I think at the same time they kinda look down their nose at talk radio."

"So why lower themselves to report about Rush Limbaugh or anybody else."

"Yeah, I think that's a problem. But beginning with our report last summer, and especially with the elections on November 8th, which talk radio did have a lot to do with – that's one place where Rush is dead on, when he says that they had some significant influence on the election, I think he's right about that – and now the mainstream media is starting to reassess, and take a closer look at the value of talk radio. And there is a lot of good talk radio. And I want to give the devil his due. Going back thirty years, that I have been a fan of talk radio, I don't think I've heard a more talented broadcaster than Rush Limbaugh, present company excepted. He's not popular because he's a demagogue, which he is, but he's popular because he's a talented broadcaster. He's really got the gift of gab."

"Carol, from uptown, you're on the air."

"Hey Bobby. Hey Mister Rendall. I see what you're saying, but I just think that you're picking on Rush. I mean, how many mistakes does Tom Brokaw or Dan Rather or those reporters make every night on the CBS news?"

"I grant you that people should go to the mainstream media, and take it with a grain of salt, and do as much as their jobs and lives afford to check out what the media tells you. But when Rush says that the New York Times never did a story on Whitewater, when the New York Times broke the Whitewater story, that's a convenient lie for him. But it's still a lie."

"Carol, thank you for the call. Gotta take a break. Gonna take a look a traffic, before we begin the drive home. Here's Rob Nelson, with MetroScan."

Edmund was waiting for me in the lobby after the show. He had discovered that a black and yellow boat dubbed The Cherokee Queen had been abandoned at the base of the Governor Nicholls Street Warf. One of his associates, disguised as a hobo, was keeping watch, while another associate was stationed at the airport with instructions to keep an eye out for a midget and a man with a wooden leg. Through other sources, Edmund had learned of a meeting that was to take place at 10:00 the next morning in front of an old abandoned theater on Magazine Street which had been converted into a furniture store. Meet me at Joey K's at 8:00, he told me. We'll have breakfast, and then see what we can find.

In the meantime, I was meeting Beverly at the hotel, where she was to be reunited with two old gradeschool and boardingschool friends. I had hoped that the two of us could be alone together. I had been thinking about that kiss on the cheek all day.

I drove to my apartment in the warehouse district. It was in an old abandoned building that had not been occupied since before the World's Fair. But with news of the casino, it was converted into a series of two and three-room rentals, with a parking lot in the rear of the building, and a pool on the roof, above the seventh floor. The apartments all had the original brick for their walls, with twelve foot ceilings and overlay pattern pine floors. My unit was a two-room on the fourth floor. It was a lot like Jeff Bridges' apartment in the Fabulous Baker Boys, with an efficiency kitchen and living space in one room, and a bedroom and bath in the other. I had a couch in the den, where I slept, with my audio and video collections, my tv set, vhs recorder, cd player, reel-to-reel tape deck, and radio. I had recordings of all of my father's old shows, as well as most of my own. I also had some Car Talk, All Things Considered, Prairie Home Companions, Howard Stern Shows, Rush Limbaugh, Hap Glaudi, David Tyree, The Shadow, The Green Hornet, Amos N Andy, London After Dark, The Town Crier,

Sidewalk Interviews, Vox Pop, Star Wars, and War of the Worlds. In addition to the radio programs, I had Richard Pryor concerts and motion picture soundtracks; I had tapes of Dylan Thomas and Jack Kerouac reading poems; and speeches by John F. Kennedy and Martin Luther King.

The other shelves were filled with videotapes and video laser discs, motion pictures and television programming. The tapes were sorted by actors, directors, writers, genres, duos, and teams. I had Robert DeNiro, for example, Stanley Kubrick, Tennessee Williams, Alfred Hitchcock, war movies, westerns, Hepburn and Tracy, Newman and Redford, Bogart and Bacall.

My bedroom, likewise, was filled with stacks of collections. I had postcards and prints, coins, stamps, and doubloons, records and books, Sugar Bowl and Super Bowl programs, Jazz & Heritage Festival posters, and collections of Life, Sports Illustrated, Newsweek, Playboy, and National Geographic magazines.

I had time to take a shower. It was cooling off a little, and the air was starting to become a little less dense. I examined my clothes as I was drying off and decided to wear an olive suit I bought at Rubenstein Brothers with an Oscar de la Renta tie. Buddy D had gotten engaged again – they were talking about it on the radio – and I was thinking about the fact that I would have to buy him a present when I realized that it would be a perfect opportunity to ask Beverly to a formal affair. I put on some after-shave, set a tape for The Simpsons, and turned off the lights. It's just a five minute drive to the hotel.

CHAPTER FOURTEEN

Beverly's friend, Stacy, was tall and skinny with long frizzy dirty blonde hair. She was wearing a baby blue-green jumpsuit with a plunging neckline, and resembled the girl that was on Three's Company between Crissy and Terry. Cindy, I think, was her name. She lived in Slidell and worked at a gardening and landscaping outfit, planting hibiscus trees and monkey grass in gas stations and fast food restaurants. She was gripping an Abita Beer bottle with her hot pink fingernails and had a ton of blue eyeshadow around the eyes.

Mary, on the other hand, was an attorney from Chevy Chase, Maryland. She was Beverly's roommate from boarding school, and was just coming out of a long and bitter divorce. She had gone to Georgetown Law School, and then got a clerkship in the Eastern District where she was hired by one of the bigger New Orleans firms. She was a short girl with a very round face and hazel eyes. She reminded me of the conversation in Taxi Driver, when Betty agrees to have pie with Travis and she is talking about the poet and the preacher and the pusher, this man of walking contradictions, in a Kris Kristoferson song. She seemed at the same time both kind and vicious, both outgoing and protective, both intelligent and naive.

"You should be a politician" she was saying, as we walked down St. Louis Street past the antique shops on our way to Bayonna. "Who do you think is running this country?" she said. "Who do you think that people trust? Ted Kennedy or Ted Koppel? Bob Novack or Bob Dole? When the President makes a speech, people don't listen to what he says, they listen to what Tom Brokaw and Cokie Roberts and George Will told you that he said. They listen to Rush Limbaugh, and Howard Stern, and around here, they listen to you." I love Cokie Roberts, I was thinking. I used to listen to her on National Public Radio, and fell in love with her voice. I always thought that I would run into her somewhere around the city. I interviewed her mother a few times, but I never got to meet her. "People hate the media" she said, "as an institution, but they love their own favorite personalities."

"But that's only because they are personalities." I told her. "That's only because we're commentators, and pundits. Editorialists. We have the luxury of sitting on the outside. When we make mistakes, it doesn't matter. Everyone remembers when we're right, but no one remembers when we're wrong."

"I don't know" she said. "I think you would be good."

Bayonna was a romantic little place on Dauphine Street. We were seated near the front of the restaurant, and immediately ordered some wine. Beverly was smashing that evening. There was this magical air about her, this aura of brass and platinum, like in those Byzantine depictions of the Virgin Mother and Child. She touched my hand with her hand under the table, and I nearly exploded every time that she smiled.

"What are y'all havin?" Stacy asked, as we started to examine the menu. The menu at Bayonna was always changing, and very eclectic and unusual in its own way. The first time I came, Tom Fitzmorris told me not to be surprised if when I looked at the menu nothing jumped out and said 'order me', but that I could pretty much just throw a dart at the menu, and whatever came up would be an excellent choice. "The pork chop is excellent" I said. (It didn't jump up and say 'order me', but I had had it before.) "I think I am going to have a filet" Mary said.

"Have you ever been to Di Piazza?"

"Where's that?"

"It's just across the street there."

"Is that the place where they just bring you those huge trays of assorted appetizers?"

"Yeah."

"Yeah, that's a great place" Mary said.

Beverly took a cigarette from her handbag, and the waiter came around with a lighter. He was a dark man with muscular features, who kinda looked like a skinnier Antonio Bandeiras, but Beverly didn't seem interested. She took a sip from her wine glass, and I noticed the red kiss of lipstick that she left on the edge of the glass and around the mouth of her cigarette. She was wearing a black sequins dress, with sheer sable stockings, and a pair of t-strap leather heels from Spain.

"So have you ever been married?" Stacy was asking.

"No" I said.

"Mary just went through a hellacious divorce."

"Do you have any kids?"

"No."

"That's good."

"Yeah, that's the one thing that I'm thankful for. Of course, now, my biological clock is ticking."

"Don't worry, doll" Stacy told her. "You've got plenty of time."

"Stacy's first love broke her heart" Beverly interjected. "She's never quite been the same."

"What did he do?" I asked her.

"See we started datin in eighth grade" she started, "and he wanted to quit school and run away and marry me. But I didn't want to quit school, and I wanted a big fancy weddin like I always dreamed about, so he went off to work and save up money to buy a house when I graduated. We used to see each other every week and stay together on the weekend. So one Friday, I went up to visit, and he leaves me a note that he has to go into Folsom to get his car fixed by his friend, this mechanic, but he would be back in a few hours and for me to wait. But I was havin a problem with my muffler, so I figured I would drive over so he could fix that too while we was there. Anyway, when I got there, no one was around. But Billy's car was there, so I knew he was there. But so Walter had this still in the back by the barn, where they made homemade moonshine and whatnot, so I figured that they were messin around out back there. So I go back, and I see these two little girls at the side of the barn, and they are laughin, laughin, laughin. So I say what's so funny. And they point. And I look over, and I see his naked butt a jigglin there in the sunlight, and I'm thinking who is this whore he's cheatin on me with and fixin to kick their butt. Then all the sudden I realized that who is he on top of, but Walter Mason, his best friend."

"Oh god."

"At least he didn't leave you for a woman."

"You think that's better?"

"Of course."

"So what's your story there Bobby?" she asked me. "How many hearts you broke?"

"None, that I know of" I said.

"Well, there's got to be someone."

"Tell us about your first love."

"My first love? Was Cathy Lee Crosby."

"No, I'm serious."

"So am I."

She did a show called That's Incredible, and I was always trying to do something incredible so that I could get on the show. Then I was in love with Joyce Davenport on Hill Street Blues. I was gonna grow up to be a police captain, like Frank Ferrilo, but then I saw her in one of those really bad made-for-tv movies and I was very disappointed. In high school, I was in love with Hope from Days Of Our Lives. I used to skip school all the time and stay home sick so that I could watch it. Then I would have a miraculous recovery, just in time to go play football after school. That summer I dated a girl for a while who reminded me of Cybill Shepherd. But she turned out to be fairly stupid, and slept around. In college, I was completely devoted to Jane Pauley. She seemed very intelligent, and pretty, and I imagined her to be the perfect mother and wife. I tried, for a year, after college, to meet Meg Ryan. I would wait outside her house and follow her to restaurants when Dennis Quaid was away shooting Tombstone, or Wyatt Earp, or whatever movie he was in. I interviewed Lynn Ganser on the radio once, and Giselle Fernandez, but neither of them seemed too interested. Then, a few years ago, I almost got married to a girl who was just like Judy Garland, but she had the same bad habits, and I was always picking her up off the floor. She said if I truly loved her, I would stay.

The Greeks have three words for love. Philia, which is a kind of companionship. Agape, which is kind of like charity. And eros, which is a longing for something beautiful, one does not have. Aristotle chose the word philia to describe man's relationship with knowledge. But Plato saw philosophy in terms of eros, the love of something beautiful, that one does not possess. And I was sitting there next to Beverly Winston, who was so inhuman that she was almost cinematic. Maybe that's why I wanted her so much.

I ordered a blackened shrimp and cornbread appetizer and a couple of garlic-honey roasted soft shell crabs. I usually find in most good restaurants that the appetizers are all excellent, and generally better than the main course. The best thing to do, therefore, is to order about three appetizers, and tell the guy to bring two of them with everyone else's meal. But since Beverly was there, I liked soft shell crabs, and I didn't want her to think I was weird.

She took my advice and got the pork chop – which I took as a sign – grilled with an interesting pear salsa and a house salad with bleu cheese dressing on the side. Stacy ordered some quail stuffed with boudin dish or something, while Mary opted for a filet topped with fresh crabmeat in a light hollandaise sauce, and another bottle of wine.

"So how do they do ratings in radio?" Mary was asking me. "I mean people are in their cars, so it's not like they can have a Nielsen box or anything."

"Well, they mostly use diaries" I explained. "They mail out these logs, and then the people are supposed to keep track of what they listen to and when. They send you a buck, I think, to get you to do it, and you do it for a week. Most of it is done by a company called Arbitron. But now they are starting to have scanners, that they can set up at the side of the road, and figure out what stations the cars are tuned to. But it's relatively new. There's not too many of them, and I'm not sure how well they work. Yet."

"My neighbor got one of those little satellite dishes" Stacy was saying. "He split off a wire and ran it over into our livin room."

"Can you get into trouble for that?"

"You can get into trouble for splicing your cable box, but I think that the dish belongs to the owner, and he can do whatever he wants."

"You don't have the kind where you have to look for the right satellite, do you?"

"I don't know" she said. "I think the neighbor got tired of my kids sittin around there all day watchin tv, that's why he did it."

"You have kids?"

"Yeah" she said. "I got three kids. Probably sittin at home watchin dirty movies on the television right now."

"Well pretty soon you're not going to need those satellite dishes or cable" Mary said. "You're just going to have one bundle of fiber optics, and then you're gonna have a central computer in your house, and it's gonna control the telephones, answering machines, cd players, video recorders, television, radio, security, video games, internet, interaction, word processing, and banking, all right there in one computer, with one fiber optics cord."

"It's kinda scary" she said.

We were starting on our third bottle of wine when they brought the appetizers. There was an elderly couple next to us, who were obviously bothered by the noise. A group of ladies were seated to the left of us, near the doorway. They were talking about whether they would ever cheat on their husbands, like in The Bridges of Madison County, and about whether they thought that their husbands were cheating on them. I noticed that one of the ladies was wearing an emerald bracelet, and I started to think about Edmund, and Frankel, and the meeting tomorrow at 10:00.

It seemed so fantastic to be chasing a midget and a one-legged man with a satchel of emeralds from South America. It was like a cross between Fantasy Island and The Fugitive.

Just then, a waiter tapped Beverly on the shoulder. She excused herself from the table and returned after several moments, grabbing her purse and saying "I'm sorry, but I have to go."

I followed her out of the restaurant and asked her if she wanted or needed me to come with her, trying to find out what was wrong. "There's been an accident, it's my grandmother" she told me. "Go back and finish your dinner. I'll see you tomorrow afternoon."

Reluctantly, I returned to the table. I told Mary and Stacy that there had been an accident. Her grandmother had suffered a stroke or a heart attack, we surmised. I started to think though, that maybe she was lying. Maybe the killers were after her. Maybe they told her not to bring anyone. Maybe she made up the story about her grandmother. Maybe she was scared. But what would they want from her, I wondered. They already had the jewels, presumably. What else could they want with Beverly.

Mary was pouring another glass of wine while the two women were laughing and drinking, telling stories about Beverly from when they knew her, and talking about men. Mary was warm and irresistible, though kind of aloof. She was wearing this royal blue sheath dress that fell about her calves, with gold and sapphire earrings and a crucifix on her neck. Her cheeks were so round, and full, like balloons, that her face looked plastic, or ceramic, like a doll, and you had to wonder what was flesh and what was bone. Her lips were full, and I wanted to kiss them. But soon my thoughts turned to Lauren Bacall, and Beverly.

"I wasn't gonna say anything, but I've got a bone to pick with you" Mary was saying. "Last week, your station was running this ad, that was sponsored by the Citizens Against Lawsuit Abuse, which is parenthetically just a secretary at State Farm. And the ad says that the personal injury lawyers are trying to get a piece of the pie with House Bill 873, which will tie judges' hands and make it harder for them to craft decisions which are fair, and easier for the personal injury lawyers to file frivolous suits. So call your Senator, and tell him to vote against House Bill 873, and tell the personal injury lawyers to get their piece of the pie someplace else. Now, you don't tell people what's in House Bill 873, you don't tell them what it says, or why it's good or bad, you just tell them to vote against the greedy personal injury lawyers."

"Well, first of all, there are a lot of FCC rules when it comes to political ads. We have to run them, regardless of their content, regardless of who the candidate is, and not only that, we have to sell it to them in any available time slot, and at the cheapest price. Plus the fact that, when it gets down to it, we are kinda like lawyers. It's not our job to agree with our sponsors, or our callers. It's only our job to provide them with an effective venue to get their message across. And if we become the censors of what they're trying to say, then anyone who isn't liked, for some reason, or who has an opinion that some might consider dangerous, or offensive, will, in effect, lose his right to be heard. Which means that the public will lose all of those perspectives, and you will have a breakdown in the marketplace of ideas."

"Yeah, but you have to at least tell people what the law says. I mean, you can put your spin on it and advocate a position, but you have to furnish people with some minimal amount of information so that they can ultimately decide for themselves. I mean, even lawyers, when they file a claim can't just say you owe me money. They have to set out the factual basis for the claim. And the lawyer who signs the pleading has to personally verify that he or she has conducted some reasonable investigation into the matter, and that there is some reasonable basis for the suit."

"Well I don't know anything about that, but in the context of the radio commercial, why can't the other side just come back and say this is what the law is about, and argue the other way?"

"Because the people who are affected by the bill don't even know that they're going to be affected, because you haven't told them what the bill's about. I mean, if Coke says that you shouldn't buy Pepsi because it has bad ingredients, then Pepsi can come back and say these are the ingredients, and they're not bad, for these reasons. And it's really just a cost of doing business. But when you're talking about a piece of legislation, it doesn't affect just Pepsi, it affects everyone. And in this case, you have a bill that prevents corporations from basically bribing people, by saying that we will pay you money if you agree not to tell anyone that our products are unsafe. So the people who are ultimately affected by the bill are all of the people that are going to go out and buy Pintos, and Pfizer heart valves, and all of the other products that are bad for you, but that you don't know anything about, in part because of these secrecy agreements, and you are forcing them to go out and spend money, to run advertisements, just so that people can have the basic fundamental information about what the law says. And I don't think that that's responsible. I don't know what the laws are on advertising when it comes to candidates, but I would imagine that this is an ad that you could refuse to air, or make them go back and change."

"That's interesting, I never thought of that, I'll check into it" I said, and poured the two ladies another glass of wine. "And it's really kind of ironic" she added, "because the bill is ultimately going to hurt you guys in the media. Because it punishes whistle-blowers, and prevents you from getting juicy information."

"Really? I don't even know what it says."

"Anyway."

"So what kind of law do you do?"

"Mostly business stuff."

"Oh, I assumed you were a personal injury lawyer."

"No, I have a CPA license, so I do a lot of tax stuff. But my nephew got killed on one of those ATVs in Mississippi, and they tried to buy the family off."

"How old was he?" asked Stacy.

"He was twelve."

"Aw, that's a shame."

All three of us were thoroughly drunk by the time that dinner arrived. Stacy was telling a joke about a minister, a priest, and a rabbi that stepped into a bar, as Mary was mounting spoons of butter onto her bread. I was studying the way that the two women organized their food before eating, and I was beginning to find both of them more interesting, and more sexual, especially Stacy. Mary was warm and maternal, passive and forbidding, with an almost religious nature, and distinctly Catholic way. Stacy, on the other hand, was lively and athletic, active and open, with a distinctly irreligious nature, and youthful way. I was thinking about Laura Dern in Wild At Heart, and I could see her taking you back to the trailer park, ripping your clothes off, and getting down on all fours. But then I pictured her kids peering in through the window, and all of my thoughts returned instantly to Beverly.

I paid the check, over Mary's objection, and we left Café Bayonna both satiated and full of wine. The three of us were heading back to the Royal Sonesta to check on Beverly. We were walking next to a buggy that was negotiating the cars and pedestrians, with the driver pointing out all of the historical landmarks and hotels, restaurants and tourist traps, museums and arcades.

The French Quarter was looking more and more like a Madonna video, with a parade of costumes and bleach blond hair and make-up popping in and out of the t-shirt shops and strip joints; stopping to watch the black kids tap dancing with bottletops stapled to their sneakers and drinking hurricanes. There were born-again Christians with giant wooden crosses who handed out fliers and yelled at people over bullhorns and Mister Microphones. The strippers and the prostitutes paced back and forth beneath the streetlamps, with men dressed as women and women dressed as men, wearing leather jackets and boots and hats and whips and chains. Every couple of blocks was an Ignatius P. Reilly at his plastic Lucky Dog stand in the shape of a hot dog, dishing out chili and onions over two-foot wieners, with band-aids dangling from their faces and blisters bubbling on their hands.

I recently saw an interview with John Goodman where someone had apparently approached him about playing Ignatius Reilly in a film version of the book, but he said that it was probably one of those books that should never be made into a movie, like A Catcher In The Rye.

Royal Street was like a completely different world, though, and Mary commented that it was like traveling from Las Vegas to Florence in one block. There were antique stores and galleries that filled all of the eighteenth century buildings, like the great districts of London, and Italy, and France.

Stacy and Mary were talking about women's clothing, and an assortment of female journalists who are for the most part impeccably dressed.

"Susan Roesgen wears nice stuff" one of them was saying.

"I like Diane Sawyer" said the other.

"Katie Couric's the best."

"Hey, have y'all ever been to DisneyWorld?" Stacy then was asking. "I wanna bring my kids to DisneyWorld."

Just then, I happened to notice two strange men, who were hobbling off like shadows into the night. One of the men was extremely short, with a tweed grey cap and flannel clothing. The other was carrying a suitcase, and limping on the sole of a wooden leg. Wait a second, I said, and followed them along the sidewalk beside the gallery windows and beneath the balconies. They turned up towards Bourbon, and I jumped behind a stationwagon that was parked beside a driveway in a no parking zone. I could hear Mary and Stacy approaching, whispering among themselves, and asking me what the hell was going on. Shhh, I whispered, and followed them with my eyes.

They paused at the corner, and surveyed the cross-street both to the left and to the right. I quickly moved across the street and kneeled behind a blue sedan. The two men crossed Bourbon Street, and I followed them past Ripley's Believe It Or Not and the Old Absinthe House to a sleazy strip joint, where they were being solicited by a bouncer at the door.

"Jesus forgives you" a man was saying, and handed me a leaflet, as I told him to get the hell out of the way, and pushed him to the side. When I looked again, finally, they were gone. I took a few steps up towards Esplanade and looked back again down the street towards Canal. There was a family of tourists from Massachusetts trying to decide whether they wanted to go into Ripley's and a couple from Texas that was asking me about Preservation Hall. Go up to St. Peter and take a right, I told them, as Mary and Stacy came up behind me, asking me what the hell was going on.

Ignoring them, I went to the strip joint and handed the guy a five dollar bill to get in. The place was dark and musty, with hot sweaty air and the stench of stale beer and urine in the walls and all over the ground. The two men I was following were seated in the front row, near the stage, where a disgusting old woman was shaking her tasseled breasts. There were a few other truck drivers and poker players next to the midget at the stage, cooing and hawing while drinking cheap bourbon and smoking bummed cigarettes. In the corner there was a young girl dancing on a table filled with kids. The obvious ring-leader was stuffing dollar bills into the stripper's panties while puffing on a fat cigar. The others looked nervous. Their hands were in their laps, and none of them had touched their beer. They were about fifteen or sixteen, I guess, and the girl who was dancing didn't look too much older than them.

Mary and Stacy had followed me into the strip bar. They were laughing and giggling, and calling a great deal of attention to themselves. "Aw, there's no men here, what a ripoff" Stacy was saying. "Yeah" Mary chimed in, "what kind of a place are you bringing us to."

"Shhh" I told them.

"What, you're trying to concentrate?"

"This is Donna Summer, I love Donna Summer" Stacy was saying.

"Do you remember Gloria Gaynor?" asked Mary, as a waitress dressed in an imitation silk teddy was approaching us from the other side. What can I get y'all, she asked us.

"Wine" Stacy told her.

"We don't have that."

"Oh, then I don't want anything."

"You have to get something. There's a one drink minimum."

"I'll have a coke."

"It's the same price as beer."

"How much is that?"

"Three-fifty."

"Three-fifty for a coke?"

"Well that includes the entertainment" she said.

"I appreciate that" said Mary. "I'll have a beer."

"Beer."

"Beer."

"Three beers."

The waitress scribbled something down on the pad and got out of the way, while the man with the wooden leg was handing a ten dollar bill to the stripper that was kneeling down at his side. "It's like, the modern world, has this national, or even global conscience" Mary was attempting to say, or something. She was really drunk by this point, and was clinging to my arm. "It's like there is no difference between real people and television characters, or movie people, or books. Like Cathy Lee Gifford."

"Crosby."

"Whatever. Isn't that what you said? And people would marry her. They would rather be at Cheers than wherever they go to, their own bars. I mean, and people know you. Right? Who you've never met. And they know you. Like they know Cliff and Norm and Sam."

"From Cheers?"

"Yes, from Cheers."

"I don't know what you're talking about" I tried to tell her, keeping my attention focused on the two men in the front row.

"It's like I was reading this book"she continued. "And he was saying that all of our knowledge is second-hand. That we know, every year, every day, more and more stuff, but that we haven't learned or experienced it first-hand. In fact, Robert Bobby Wilson, I bet that there is almost nothing that you actually know. That's not from movies or books or tv. And, but, we have a national conscience. A shared conscience, of facts, characters, events, titles, episodes, ideas. Which are familiar. Recognizable. And which no one before electricity could have ever anticipated or conceived."

"I don't know" I said. "I guess so." I didn't know what the hell she was talking about, and by that point, I really didn't care to place too much effort into trying to figure out what she was trying to say.

The waitress returned with the beer, as Stacy and Mary haggled over who was going to pay, so that by the time the waitress moved out of the way, the two men I was following were gone. I looked around the room and noticed a black velvet curtain that was flapping in the back of the strip joint, on the other side of the bar.

I sprung up from my chair and made my way through the chairs and the tables, lunging through the curtain and into a dimly lit passageway. I came towards the end of the hallway, where it was quiet and dark. There was no one around, and I could no longer hear the music from the main part of the bar. Some dirty pictures were glued to the walls, and there was a mirror on the ceiling, which ran to the end of the hall where there were these big, refrigerator or freezer-like steel doors. I opened the door on the right, where the midget was standing there with his arms folded across his chest; he had a large grin on his face, with the suitcase at his feet. The other man was waiting for me at the door.

CHAPTER FIFTEEN

When I woke up, I didn't know where I was. My head was banging and throbbing with sharp pains that shot through the base of my neck and behind my ear. My eyes focused on a doorway, where through the opening I saw a naked woman who was standing at a dresser, dabbing perfume gently against her wrists and on her neck. She took a gold crucifix from her dresser, swept her hair back behind her shoulders, and fastened the chain, while the gold cross descended among her round and naked breasts. The woman touched her stomach, and then stepped behind the doorway, where she disappeared.

There was an armoire to the right, with a television and a stereo, and I realized that I was lying on a sofa in the middle of Mary's den. I could hear the morning radio show in the background from her bedroom, and listened to the overlapping sounds of an automated Krups coffee and espresso machine. When Mary returned to the dresser she was wearing a black lace push-up with a pair of black bikini panties that were snug against her bottom. There was a garter belt about her waist, which was fastened to a silky pair of hose.

She stepped into a knife-pleated skirt, and started to button a silk blouse over her bra. I closed my eyes and pretended I was asleep, until she sat beside me with a cup of coffee, and started to stroke my hair. I opened my eyes, and pretended to wake, saying where am I, what happened, and all that kind of stuff.

"Some man attacked you in the strip joint" she told me. "He struck you with something over the head."

"Did they catch him?"

"No, he disappeared, we didn't know what happened. Then this guy helped me get you back here."

"Thank you" I said.

"How are you feeling? Do you want some coffee?"

"Yes" I thanked her, "thank you very much."

"Who were those guys?" she asked me. "Why were we chasing them?"

"I think they have something that belongs to Beverly."

"What?"

"Don't worry about it, it doesn't matter" I told her, taking the coffee mug and using it to warm my hands. I'm sorry I brought you into that place, I told her. I feel like Dustin Hoffman in The Graduate, or Robert DeNiro in Taxi Driver.

"That's okay" she said, "I was so drunk. I didn't care."

"Well, let me get out of your hair" I said. "You probably need to go to work, and I probably need to take a shower."

As I sat up, though, I noticed that Mary was wearing a silver bracelet on her ankle, with a large scissor-cut emerald dangling on its side. "I never noticed that last night" I told her. "Where did you get it?"

"From a man" she told me. "He was my first lover. We had an affair when I was very young."

"What was his name?" I asked her.

"Frankel" she said. "Henry Frankel. I haven't seen him in years."

Edmund and I were crouched in a balcony across the street from the furniture store, kneeling among the potted bougainvillea trees and some ferns. The sky was dark and full of clouds, and it looked like it was going to rain. My head was still banging and throbbing behind the ear, and the skin was very tender, so that I could even feel the weight of my hair. When Mary left for work I went home and took a shower. I took a few aspirin, and then met Edmund for breakfast at Joey K's. I told him about everything that had happened. He didn't seem overly concerned.

It was always a pleasure talking to Edmund. He had an eclectic array of interests, and could speak intelligently about every sort of topic, from medieval pottery to intergalactic communication. That morning, in addition to the case, we talked about miracle plays, Stradivarius violins, the Buddhism of Ceylon, World War I tanks, and World War II planes. Nevertheless, there was a gap in much of our communication.

Edmund didn't seem to share my interest in politics, nor in radio, film, and tv. I guess he was more of a Puritan. Kinda like those Hawthorne characters from the nineteenth century.

In any event, we were waiting there for this supposed meeting. I'm still not sure how Edmund found out about it, nor who was going to be there, nor what did it mean. Edmund had one of those sound guns, like the ones Gene Hackman used in The Conversation. There was a woman at the corner who was telling her kids that they better mind her and trying to zip up the little girl's raincoat before it rains. She was a cute little girl, with pig tails and a Sesame Street knapsack. Her brother was making faces and trying to walk along the curb as if it were a balance beam. There was another man saying I can't believe you're drinkin so early, and a couple from Minnesota who was trying to decide how much money they could spend on furniture and antiques. I love the rug, the woman was saying, but I don't want to spend three thousand dollars on something that, if the kids spill some kool-aid or the dog goes to the bathroom, it will be destroyed.

There was kind of a mysterious man on the corner. He wasn't mysterious in a ghostly or supernatural way, he was just mysterious in that he didn't really seem to belong. He was a dark man, with dark eyes, and white white hair. He was dressed in an expensive pinstripe, with a Rolex gold watch on his wrist. And he seemed to be waiting for someone.

When it began to rain, it was harder to hear with the sound guns. The street had cleared out a bit and was fairly empty, save a few cars that were returning from downtown. What time is it? I wondered.

"About 10:15."

"They're late" I said. "You think they're coming?"

"Yes."

"Did you see those kids down the street with the blue bandannas?" I asked him. "I think they were Seventh Ward Posse, or something."

"I didn't notice them."

"I think they left when it started raining" I said.

"My concern right now is with that tall black gentlemen on the corner" Edmund was saying.

"Yeah, I noticed him too" I said. "He looks like he's waiting for someone."

"Or two people" Edmund said.

We waited there a few more minutes, and I was watching a woman who reminded me of Natalie Wood. Not the Rebel Without A Cause Natalie Wood, or the Westside Story Natalie Wood, or the Natalie Wood that was in Gypsy. But the black-and-white Natalie Wood. Love With A Proper Stranger. She was loading house plants into the back of her sport-utility vehicle and drinking Mellow Yellow from a plastic bottle. The rain was dancing softly against the skin of her windbreaker, as drops began to bead along the edges of her face. She finished loading the plants and took one last sip before wiping her lips and tossing the bottle into a nearby garbage can.

Then I saw them. They were coming from downtown, with the midget carrying the satchel, and the man on one leg hobbling behind. "There they are" I tapped Edmund, and put my headphones back on.

They made their way to the furniture store, and then stopped. They were still two buildings over from our suspect and I started to think that maybe we had been wrong. I thought I saw the midget say something to the other guy, but I was listening attentively and didn't hear a thing.

The midget had dark skin, with a giant freckle on his forehead and a giant gap between his two front teeth. His hair was thick, and parted, so that it looked like he was wearing a wig. The taller man resembled Inspector Cluseau from the old Pink Panther movies. He was awkward and clumsy, with pale white skin. He was wearing a pair of tinted glasses and a felt hat which dipped down over his brow.

The two waited there for a moment, and then glided sideways toward our suspect, while our suspect glided sideways in the other direction towards them. The three men nodded to one another.

"All settled?" I think the black gentleman said.

The midget nodded and placed what must have been an emerald into his hand. The man inspected the gemstone. "When?"

"By night" the midget answered.

Something "a pier" I think the man said, "three to the right of the bridge."

"Then there's just the matter of our deposito" said the man with the wooden leg.

"Of course" the darker man said. "Follow me to my car."

"Come on, lets go" Edmund grabbed me, and we speeded down the stairs. When we got to the doorway, the three men were standing behind a black Mercedes. The trunk was open, and the man was grabbing what appeared to be a briefcase from inside.

Immediately I was recognized by the midget. He pointed, and said something, and the three men bounded into an old building, where they disappeared.

Edmund and I followed them into the converted theater, which was hollow and dark, with dressers and tables and chairs haphazardly placed about the room. Edmund had a thirty-eight revolver. I myself was unarmed. The two of us crept over to the east side of the building and took shelter in a hollow space behind an armoire. I thought I heard something behind us. But when I turned, no one was there.

Our three suspects, at that point, were making their way around back to the entrance. I could see the top of a felt hat and the tall man's white hair. I alerted Edmund, and we circled around to the base of a large sleigh-like bed.

It was just like the end of one of those movies, when the cops follow the criminals to the warehouse or the factory or the refinery, and then they lose their gun, and then they get captured or almost get captured or killed, and then the woman pops out of nowhere and shoots the bad guy in the head. But in this case, of course, there wasn't any woman. Except Beverly. And I could not picture her handling a gun.

In any case, Edmund stood and said halt, pointing his revolver at the larger man's chest. The midget drew his own gun and fired. He missed, and Edmund fired back, striking a mirror. The midget fired again and the three men scuffled to the door. Edmund followed them cautiously, and I waited there for a few minutes, shitting in my pants.

A few minutes later, I caught up with Edmund, who was at the doorway. The three men were at the black Mercedes. We were approaching, as they were attempting to unlock the door. Just then, three young kids approached the driver, demanding his brief case and his watch.

"Give it up."

I turned, and one of the other kids with the blue bandannas was pointing a gun at my head. "Put the piece down, fatso" he told Edmund. "Lest you wanna see your boy's brains spattered all over that stupiddy-ass suit."

As Edmund was slowly placing his gun on the sidewalk, we heard some shots being fired, and when we turned, we saw the street kids shooting the man in the suit and taking his briefcase. The midget returned fire, hitting two of the kids in the side.

Our attacker took a few shots at the midget and the man with the wooden leg as they jumped into the Mercedes, while the fourth kid with the Rolex watch and the briefcase was running away. I had thrown my wallet and keys on the ground, but the boy had forgotten about us and was already gone.

"Are you okay?" Edmund asked me.

"Oh my god," I was on the sidewalk trying to catch my breath.

"You okay?" he asked me again.

"Oh my god" I said.

"I guess it's gonna be a little bit harder to find them, now."

"Have fun" I said. "You can find them by yourself."

"It's a lot different than watching it on tv there, huh fella?" he teased me.

"I think I'm gonna die."

I could start to hear the sirens from the ambulances and the police cars approaching from Jackson Avenue. "By tonight" he said, "you'll be ready to get after them again."

"Hobbies are peculiar things, some more so than others.

"As a kid, mine were different from my sisters and my brothers.

"Some people collect stamps, or coins, or flags, from far and near.

"Others collect baseball cards, or cans that once held beer.

"Some collections must be bought, you have to be a buyer.

"But this is not at all the case with Vernon Nietermeyer....

I was in the booth with my two guests. They were drinking coffee and getting used to their headphones, while I was watching the clock. We had about fifty seconds. When does Rush actually come on, they were asking me. He comes on about 10:00 in the morning, and we tape him, along with the segments from Paul Harvey and Charles Osgood, which is what we are listening to now, and then we engineer them together, along with the spots, on tape delay from 1:00 to 4:00.

"Because of his collection, people call him Doctor Rot.

"But he insists that what he has in actuality does not.

"Someone gave him kiwi fruit, or watermelon which fermented.

"And day by day he noticed that the office became scented

"With a smell, says Nietermeyer, not garbagy or sewery.

"Oh no, he says, it smells more like a winery or brewery.

"Some might say that this is a hobby you can keep,

"But Nietermeyer likes it though, he says it's fun and cheap.

"Some food may get ripe and gooey for a little while, it's true.

"But c'est las vie, the French might say, and chaque un a son gout.

The Osgood File. I'm Charles Osgood, on the CBS Radio Network."

"Good evening ladies and gentlemen, this is Robert Wilson, and we are here today with Kevin Kimball, a former president of the American Trial Lawyers Association, and one of the lead attorneys on what is now the largest class action in American history. In the last forty years, there have been over 813 claims against the cigarette companies, who have lost only twice, and both of those losses were overturned on appeal. But with reports that the tobacco companies have known since the early 1960s that nicotine is addictive and have been manipulating the levels in their cigarettes to keep smokers hooked, over fifty law firms from around the country have banded together for a massive class action which was filed last summer in the Eastern District in New Orleans. On the other side of the coin, we have Connie McNamara, who is the current president of the New Orleans Bar Association, and who represents Philip Morris, one of the nation's largest cigarette manufacturers. She maintains that people are responsible for their own actions, and that smokers assume the risks for any sickness or death that might ensue. Kevin, why don't we start with you. Tell us a little bit about the suit."

"Thanks Robert. And thanks for having me. I think the first point I'd like to make is that we're not trying to outlaw cigarettes. We're not trying to ban smoking. We're just saying that cigarettes cause four hundred thousand deaths per year, along with countless other health problems, which result in very real economic as well as human consequences; and, as a result, under our legal system, the manufacturers of those products are responsible for at least part of the damages they cause. And so, forgetting, for a moment, about all of the perjury and the deception and the nicotine manipulation and the toxic additives and the targeting of children, regardless of the moral issues, it's an economic matter. The cigarette companies are reaping one hundred percent of the profits, and assuming none of the liability."

"Well, Mister Kimball says that he wants to ignore those so-called moral issues of assumption of risk, and personal responsibility, but those issues cannot be ignored. People who smoke know that they may become ill, and yet they choose to assume that risk, by smoking anyway. Then they come back, years later, and say, we are not responsible, you are. Which is indicative of this age where no one is willing to take responsibility for the things they do. We live in a free society, where people make personal choices, based on calculated risks. Then, when things don't go our way, we look to someone else, and claim that we are not responsible. It's my fathers fault, because he molested me. It's my husband's fault, because he abused me. It's society's fault, because it ignored me. People make choices. And they have to live with those choices. It's part of being human. It's part of living in a free society."

"You are absolutely correct. People should take responsibility for their actions. Philip Morris and RJR and the American Tobacco Company make a choice to addict people to a deadly product. That's how they make their money. They could be in business doing something else. But that's what they choose to do. And with that choice, comes responsibility. And I find it highly ironic that the tobacco industry is trying to invoke this nation of victims defense, when the tobacco industry is just about the biggest self-proclaimed victim around. Constantly whining about how they are the poor, innocent, helpless, multi-billion dollar victims of a hostile media, a biased medical and scientific community, a power-hungry FDA, and greedy trial lawyers, and trying to do everything they can to evade their own mantra of personal responsibility."

"But it's not our responsibility. It's the consumer's choice. It's the consumer's health. And it's the consumers responsibility, if they get sick, because that have assumed the risk of smoking."

"Well I didn't. I don't buy cigarettes. I don't smoke cigarettes. And I sure as hell don't profit from the sale of cigarettes. And yet, when cigarettes cause cancer, when cigarettes cause emphysema, when cigarettes cause heart disease, I am expected to pick up the tab. Every year, non-smokers, as well as smokers, are forced to pay billions of dollars in health insurance premiums, and medical expenses, to cover the costs of smoking. And not only that, but we also pay in the form of disability benefits, and workers compensation benefits, social security benefits, welfare, medicare, and medicaid. Not to mention the human costs. Every year, over four hundred thousand people die from cigarette-related disease. Four hundred thousand. And the cigarette companies say that's not our problem. Why not? They know that cigarettes kill. They know that nicotine is addictive. They manipulate the levels. They add ammonia, and other toxins, which make something already dangerous even more harmful and more addictive. And nevertheless they accept 48 billion dollars each year in revenues, for a product which they know will kill you, and then refuse to pay a single penny for the damages they cause. Not one cent."

"We gotta take a break" I said. "But we will be right back, with a response from Connie McNamara, and we will take your calls, with Robert Wilson, right here, on your News Talk and Saints Radio, WWL 870 AM."

CHAPTER SIXTEEN

I was waiting for Edmund in the station lobby. Tonia was still there, waiting for her husband to come and pick her up, while talking to one of the delivery boys. She was just like Ava Gardner in Night Of The Iguanas. An older woman, full-figured, with dark hair, full lips, brilliant eyes, and a very warm smile. Her husband worked for Ford or Cadillac or one of those big American car companies. He goes around to all of the dealerships giving lectures on customer service, sales, and repairs. The two of them moved to Montgomery for a while, but she didn't like it that much, and when they moved back to New Orleans, she came back to the station.

"Did you see Michael Jackson?" she was asking.

"Yeah, he's a freak" the deliveryman said.

"If you look at what he looked like when he was a kid, to now, there is no resemblance. None whatsoever."

"He doesn't look human" the deliveryman said. "He looks like he's wearing a mask."

"He says he wants to go back to his childhood" Tonia told him.

"If I had all that money, I'd forget about my childhood. I'd forget about my adulthood, puberty, and all that."

"I wouldn't want to be famous, though" she said. "You couldn't go anywhere."

"That's why these guys got it so good, right Bobby? Stick to radio."

Edmund and I had determined that our friends were going to attempt to leave the country by water, sailing out into the Gulf through Lake Borgne and Lake Pontchartrain. Sure enough, one of Edmund's associates had discovered a boat on the lakefront at the edge of the marina registered by a Jonathan Small under the flag of Panama and bearing the name, in roman letters, The Four. There was no one on board, at the time, so Edmund's associate remained on watch at the marina after procuring a boat from one of the local weekend fishermen, while I waited for Edmund and Beverly.

I was reading an interview with Tom Cruise, who was talking about Born On The Fourth of July, and how Ron Kovic and Oliver Stone and all of these guys went off to Vietnam thinking that they were going to be John Wayne. Then they came home paralyzed, and impotent, like Jake in The Sun Also Rises, trying to figure out how to be a man. He felt very strongly about the subject matter, and so he agreed to do the film with a deferred payment plan, which essentially meant, for free. Nobody ever knows what is going to hit it big at the box office, he was saying. So you better do something that you believe in; because if it's not financially successful, you have got to make sure that you walk away with something. That was his philosophy.

To some people, a philosophy is a belief. Like a credo, or a mantra, or a quote. But I have found that philosophy is more of a process, a dialectic, a becoming. Which is why Socrates was the first and greatest of philosophers, because he discovered that it's not so much in the answer, as in the questioning. Philosophy is translation. It is a process of naming, and defining, and redefining, and shaping, and reshaping. Searching for the symbols, and the analogies. Segregating events and ideas from the masses, and seeing them as they are. Or taking the particular, and making it universal, and comprehensible to us all. Philosophy is not a thought, but a way of thinking. That is my philosophy.

In any event, I didn't know why I was waiting for Edmund. At first it was because of Beverly, but it wasn't about Beverly anymore. I felt like I had been swept up into this great something, like Robert Redford in Three Days Of The Condor, or Cary Grant in North By Northwest. I wasn't scared. I wasn't worried. I wasn't hopeful. I just couldn't wait to see what would happen next.

CHAPTER SEVENTEEN

When Beverly wasn't around, I could hear the echo of her voice. It was like the wind blowing over the remains of some ancient continent, reminding you of everything that had ever been beautiful and now gone. But in her presence, the sound of her voice was usurped by her visual image. Even casual, as she was now, Beverly had that magical Audrey Hepburn quality about her, and seemed appareled in the rarest of fabrics, and most eloquent of hues.

Edmund, on the other hand, was blowing his nose into a soiled handkerchief. He was wearing one of his seersucker suits, (this time gray and white rather than blue), with his white Dexter bucks and a silly strawberry tie. We were on the deck of a thirty-four foot double-engine motorboat, keeping an eye on The Four from an nearby pier. It was a smaller boat, about thirty feet, with an outboard motor and two black racing stripes on the side.

Edmund's associate was wearing a Southern Yacht Club t-shirt with cut-off jeans and was pretending to hose down the slip. His name was Jeff, and had just resigned from the NOPD. It's too black and political, he said. Yeah, well, Edmund reminded him, it had always been too white and political in the past. Of course that doesn't make it right, was my opinion. It's like all of those To Kill A Mockingbird trials that Bob Dylan wrote songs about in the sixties, like The Lonesome Death Of Hattie Carrol or The

Death Of Emmit Till, where all-white all-male juries would refuse to convict their white peers for killing black people, but that doesn't make it okay for black juries to do the same.

In any event, Jeff was short and thin, with dark hair and wild grey eyes. He wore a diving watch on his left hand. On his right hand was a leather bracelet that his wife brought back from Mexico when they were in the eighth grade at Holy Name. He brushed the leather strap against his chin as he was washing down the pier with a yellow hose. Edmund, meanwhile, was pretending to flush out the engine, while Beverly and I were lying together in the cabin, listening to the radio.

Her hips were lithe and graceful, and seemed aroused by the touch of my fingers along the rim of her jeans. My other hand was wrapped about her fingers, clutched beneath the weight of her excited nipples and against her breast. Her hair smelled like apricots and consumed my senses, as the quiet sounds of her breathing grew louder and louder over time. All of the sudden though, Edmund called out "they're here", and she stood up, letting go of my hand. I will never forget the image of her standing in the galleyway, fresh and awake, and ready to be born.

The two suspects spent little time warming up the engine. I didn't see any kind of suitcase or satchel, but Edmund's associate assured us that the emeralds were on board. The taller man with the amputated leg was working the engine, as the dwarf-like figure unfastened the cleats and they backed out of the slip and into the channel. We were docked on the far side of an adjacent pier, and watched them make their way down the line of boathouses and rocks protecting the manmade harbor from the waves. We backed out of our slip and followed them through the marina, passing a few of the larger sailboats who were coming into the yacht club and the white Coast Guard house next to Bart's on the right. As soon as they got past the last of the channel buoys, the man with the wooden leg shifted their boat into full throttle, and steered her off to the east.

"She's fast" Jeff was saying, as we headed out towards the north and around this really large fishing boat, before meandering back over to the southeast, and following closely at the edge of their wake. The hum of the engines was almost lyrical. I watched the bow of the boat cutting across the water, and forgot momentarily what we were doing and even where I was.

"You didn't tell me that you had almost been killed" Beverly then said to me, and I suddenly remembered where I was and who we were following.

I was afraid, at the time, I admit. But such fear, I think, was instinctive, and for the most part biological. Because death, to me, as a concept, has never been real. You know what I mean? I mean, I have always thought of life as being absolute, and one-dimensional. As long as I am living, there is life. You know what I'm saying? And when you're dead, that's it, the show's over, but the dead never know.

"I think we're gaining a little."

"They can't go any faster" Edmund said. "They must know that we are after them."

"Yeah, we should catch up to them in a few minutes" Jeff said.

Just then, however, I noticed that a small ketch with no lights was sliding into our path from the north. The captain probably couldn't see us, because they were flying a pretty big jenny, which obstructed his view; but even if they could see us, there was really nothing they could do about it, because the wind was coming from the west, and he was headed up about as far as he could go. Watch out! I called, and Edmund's associate started to steer the boat away from the sailboat, but Beverly shouted no, we were too close to the shore.

Jeff slammed the wheel all the way to the port side, as far as it would possibly go, and the boat started to skid, almost, or hydroplane, toward the sailboat, as the force of the turn threw Edmund and I over the chairs. I prepared for the impact, trying to grab Beverly, but we missed the sailboat by a matter of inches and found ourselves heading out towards the center of the lake. Edmund asked if everyone was okay, as he brushed off his jacket. Beverly seemed a bit nervous and started to squeeze my hand. Jeff steered the boat back on course, but we had lost a lot of valuable ground.

It was a clear night, full of moonlight and plenty of stars. Though the air was moist and heavy, you couldn't feel it with all the wind, and we started to relax again. The two men were like shadows on the smaller vessel. It was like something out of Johnny Quest or one of those Sunday morning newspaper cartoons. We were gaining on them, yard by yard. When we got close, Edmund tried to turn the spotlight on, but it had disconnected in the fray.

The midget had been perched on the bow, like a look-out, but started to make his way back to the cockpit where the other man was steering the boat. It appeared to us, through the darkness, that the two cartoon figures had begun to scuffle. Edmund took out his gun and fired a warning shot in the air, but The Four continued erratically on its way.

After a few minutes we lost sight of the two figures, as the boat began to slalom among the broken piers and wood pilings at the edge of the lake. We had to slow down in order to negotiate the pilings, and eventually decided to slip out towards the middle, and track them from the open water.

At some point we thought we heard a gunshot in the distance, but at that point, we could not tell.

We followed the sound of the motorboat's engines for ten or fifteen minutes, and then noticed a distinct change in pitch to their hum.

"Stop for a second" Edmund said.

Jeff turned down the throttle, and we came to rest in a spot just off the point. We could hear the frogs and the crickets, but our suspect's engines had clearly stalled.

"You think it's a trap?" Jeff wondered.

"I don't know" Edmund replied.

"What if we go in looking for them, and we get stuck, and then they speed away?"

"That's the same thing I was thinking."

"Was that a gunshot we heard?"

"I don't know."

"Could have been the engine, or something."

"Well lets not just sit around and wait here."

"Okay" Edmund agreed. "Lets go on ahead."

Jeff put the engines back into low gear, and we glided into the reeds. We were somewhere past the Lakefront Airport, and in the distance you could hear the echo of car engines on I-10. The sounds of the insects and amphibians grew louder, but after several moments, I thought I heard someone beginning to moan. "Shhh" I said, "lower the engines. Is that someone moaning?"

"Sounds like it" Beverly said. "Sounds like it's coming from over there."

"Help me" a man coughed in the distance. Instantaneously, I recognized The Four. It was trapped in the reeds. Jeff and Edmund had their guns drawn, Jeff a rifle, Edmund his thirty-eight. "Put your hands over your head" said Jeff, as Edmund asked where the midget was.

"Help me" the man said, "please help me, I've been shot."

"Where is your friend?"

"I don't know" he said.

The boat had become stranded on a sandbar, and the man had been thrown out into the reeds. Jeff placed handcuffs on the man's wrists, and made a tourniquet with his belt, to wrap around the wounded thigh of our suspect's half-wooden leg. "This piece aint been too good a luck for you, has it there fella" said Jeff, as the man said "it's my white whale."

"Where are the emeralds?" I asked him.

"There, in the satchel, under that seat."

As Jeff helped the man back into the boat, I lifted the vinyl matting, where the metal lock had been broken on the door to the fiberglass compartment below. There was a black leather satchel, the same satchel we had seen on Magazine Street earlier that day. I lifted it out of the compartment and placed it on the deck, beside Beverly. Together we opened the case. But there was nothing inside.

We took the man back to the marina, and waited for an ambulance to arrive. We had searched all over for the midget, but couldn't find him anywhere. We had also searched the boat for the emeralds, but they too appeared to be gone. The man with one leg was still handcuffed and wrapped with a tourniquet, propped on a couple of vinyl seat covers that we had set out next to our slip on the wooden pier. Edmund had brought some whiskey, and we had poured it out over his wound.

The man was dark, and foreboding, with deep hollow temples and solemn brown eyes. They crawled beneath his eyelids and seemed like they could turn white or red at any time. The man had these ears that were large and hairy, and had long hairs descending from his nose. There was blood on his arms and legs, and on the pier below.

"I didn't kill that Frankel bastard" he said. "That was the midget's idea."

"I know" Edmund said, handing him the bottle of whisky. "You were still trying to make your way up the rope."

"How did you know that?" he said, and then it doesn't matter. "It's not important" he told us. "I thought that he had gone to bed. The lights were off, except for in the kitchen. I though that he had gone to bed."

The man had somewhat of a Spanish accent, but you could tell that he was uniquely American. He had that Vietnam age bitterness about him, like Jonathan Rambo in First Blood. His voice though, was compelling, like Raul Julia's or Anthony Quinn's, and it was a pleasure, despite his mangled appearance, to follow his tones.

"How did you know that the gems had been discovered?" Edmund wondered.

"It doesn't matter, not now, it doesn't matter now" he said. "I would have killed his father, I admit that. I would have killed him in a heartbeat. But it wasn't his fault that he was Frankel's son."

"So who's the midget?" Jeff asked him.

"Chesley."

"Chesley what?"

"Chesley Alford."

"And he obviously has the emeralds."

"Let him keep them" the man said. "They have been nothing but an albatross around my neck, a curse upon me, for the last twenty years. I spent the first half of my life diggin ditches in Segovia, and now I'm gonna spend the second half making license plates in Angola. And for what? A bunch of green rocks. I wish I never heard of the goddamn Neiva collection. I have been a slave to it since that bastard held a knife to my neck twenty years ago. And every poor sucker that's come into contact with it seems to be cursed with death."

"How did you come to meet with my father?" asked Beverly. "And what is the Sign of Four?"

"In a second, let me catch my breath" the man said, "then I will tell you everything." He took a few sips from the whiskey bottle, and Edmund offered him a dry cigar. The man bit off the end and had Edmund's associate light it for him. He took a few deep puffs, and then started to tell us his tale. "My best friend from high school, Ernesto, his mom was from Cartagena, beautiful woman, mind you, and he still had family there. I knew a little Spanish and he spoke both Spanish and Portuguese, which are actually pretty different – Portuguese is more like Italian – and but so anyway, we were gonna go down after graduation, stay with his family for a while, travel around, go hiking in the Andes, head over to Rio for Carnival, drink some coffee, do some drugs. After a while, though, we ran out of money, and we both got jobs in the mountains on this coffee plantation. The guy that owned the place was friends with Ernesto's aunt, I think they were lovers, and so anyway he gave us these real cushy jobs, riding around on horses and making sure that the peasants were out there working hard in the fields. We had it pretty good then. We had a pretty nice cabin. We had the best coffee, and the best drugs, and there was this little town nearby that had these great cheap little restaurants and shops and bars. The country-side was beautiful, and I thought that I could live there forever as a coffee planter for the rest of my life.

"After a few months, though, the peasants from all around the region started to revolt. It was the typical bullshit Marxist class-warfare thing, that had probably gone on for centuries and centuries. Every night you could see the fires, and there were bands of vagrants with guns and sticks and whatnot wandering over the plantations and through the towns. My boss, however, was an obstinate man. He sat out on his veranda, drinking pisco and smoking Cuban cigars. He thought that nothing could or even would try to harm him. But he was wrong.

"Ernesto pleaded with me that we should leave. And I would have, but I was in love with the plantation owner's wife. She was a gorgeous woman. We would meet in the middle of the night beside a stream, and go skinny-dipping, and lie until morning. I could not leave her there to be raped and slaughtered by a bunch of dirty peasants, so I stayed.

"One night, I heard gunshots in the distance. I raced to the house, but when I got there, it was too late. She was lying in the mud, all beaten and torn, with the clothes ripped from her back, and blood all down her face. Her husband was dead also. He died with a gun in his hand. He had taken three or four peasants with them, who were still bleeding on the road. When I looked at her again, I flew into a rage. I rode off to find the animals which had done this, with Ernesto following behind. He was yelling at me to stop. It's not worth it, you'll get yourself killed, he said.

"Unfortunately, however, I got Ernesto killed. I only lost my leg. Ernesto pulled me to safety after I fainted from the shock, and made a tourniquet. He had been shot in the belly, and was bleeding. By the time I woke up, he was dead.

"After I got out of the hospital, I hobbled around a bit. I thought about coming back to the states, but I had this wooden stick here as my nub, and every time I looked down at it I was ashamed. Anyway, finally, I landed a job at this hotel in a town called Quibdo. It was a fairly nice joint, right on the river. I worked with these three natives who mostly spoke Spanish. So I had some contact with them, but they pretty much kept to themselves.

"One night, I was standing out in front of the hotel. There was an old whore trying to entice the local teenagers across the street, and I was enjoying a fat cigar, when all of the sudden, my co-workers grabbed me. Arturo was holding a knife to my throat, as Jaime pinned my shoulders back against the wall. At first I thought they might be part of some revolution or something. 'Be quiet' Arturo said. 'Don't make a sound.'

"'Either you will swear by God Jesus Christ that you will join us forever, or we will throw your dead body into a ditch. You have ten seconds to decide.'

"How can I decide if you don't tell me what you want me to do? I asked them.

"'If you pledge yourself this night, we will swear by this knife and by the threefold oath which no honorable man has ever been known to break, that you shall share in the greatest treasure you can ever imagine. A quarter of the collection shall be yours.'

"Okay, I said. It was, as Don Corleone says, an offer I couldn't refuse.

"'Then you will swear by the honor of your family, by the flag of your countrymen, and by the cross of your Lord, Jesus Christ, that you will speak no word against us now or in the future.'

"I swear it, I said. And from that moment forward, the four of us would forge a sacred bond of friendship, badged by this sign, The Sign of Four."

Small lifted up his shirt sleeve where the same swastika-like symbol which had appeared on the parchment beside their names was cut into his skin, like a crude and novice tattoo. "Arturo and Jaime explained" he continued, "that there was a very wealthy plantation owner in Neiva, who had mines in the east, and had gathered the most exclusive collection of emeralds in the world. The man was dying, however, and there were rumors that the government was going to expropriate his land when he was dead, leaving his son with nothing. So the old man attempted to use the gemstones as a bartering chip, to bribe the politicians. He sent his most trusted servant with some of the stones to the politicians in Bogota, but he removed the very best gems from his collection, and was sending them secretly to his son, who was living in a small townhouse on the coast. On his travels, the man who was carrying the emeralds was attacked by a band of peasants, but Arturo's cousin, Paulito, saved his life. Paulito promised to help the man get to the coast safely, and they were to arrive in Quibdo that night. Paulito would lead the poor bastard to the hotel, where we would knock him over the head, and take the loot.

"A few hours later, they showed up at the hotel. I was supposed to stand guard, to hold up any visitors in the lobby, while my comrades took the guy into the kitchen and did the dirty work. Paulito came in first. He was a big man, with a long neck and a single thick brow. The other guy was short. He looked small and weak, and I couldn't understand why someone would have sent him. On the other hand, maybe that was part of the disguise. In any case, I gave him a room, and then went to the front door of the hotel, lighting a cigar.

"After a few minutes, I heard a scuffle, and the little man came running down the stairs. He grabbed my shirt and begged me to help him. My wooden leg gave way, and I fell. Before I could think straight, Arturo had grabbed the little guy, and shoved a knife into his side.

"My comrades buried the body in the basement of the hotel, in a wall, and we immediately hid the treasure, each vowing that our actions would be for the benefit of the four. All for one, and one for all. This was the Sign of Four.

"What we didn't realize was that the plantation owner sent a servant to spy on the courier, who soonafter realized that the man and the treasure had disappeared. We were arrested, and tried, and stuck in a Colombian jail, where the four of us became very close. Like brothers. We played cards, and talked about what it was going to be like when we got out. How we were gonna live, and all of the things we were gonna buy and all that. But then they separated us. And I was cold, and achy, and alone. Every day pressed on me like the weight of a thousand years. I had killed Ernesto. I had lost my one true love. I was a cripple. And I was going to spend the rest of my life in a miserable Colombian jail.

"Then one day, two Americans arrived. They had fought together in Vietnam, and then spent a few years hunting crocodiles and snakes in Brazil. They were making their way back to America, when this guy Frankel ran up a bunch of gambling debts with the locals. He apparently had a lot of money back in the states, but had some trouble getting his hands on it down there, and so they made a deal to work as guards in the prison until the debts were paid. Anyway, I got to be friends with them. And I decided to cut a deal. I sent word for authority from my three companions, and they agreed that if Frankel and Winston would help us escape, they could divide an equal share.

"From what I understand, Frankel wanted to split the jewels with Winston, pay off their gambling debts, take off, and leave us in jail. But Winston wanted to honor his word. They got into an argument, and the next night Frankel slipped off, found the treasure, and ran away with it back to America.

"Meanwhile, I rotted in jail for fifteen years, while a lust for vengeance was growing inside of me, day after day, hour by hour. My Colombian friends on the other side of the prison were not treated so well, and over time, each of them died. When I finally escaped, I hopped a freighter to America, and Chesley, who was a stevedore from Scotland, saved me from the captain and stowed me away. He brought me food, and kept me well-hid, and I figured that since everyone else was dead, I had the authority to let him in on half the loot. When we got to America, we discovered that Winston was dead, and that Frankel was dying. We went out to his plantation house, where he was supposed to be. We peered through the window, and the old bugger had a heart attack right there and died. I pinned the Sign of Four to his chest, but it became obvious that Frankel died without telling anyone where the collection was hidden.

"Me and Chesley went around playing Barnum and Bailey for a while, but we were always checking in on the Frankel boys, waiting for them to find the emeralds, and taking our share. We didn't know it would take another ten or fifteen years for those bastards to find it. I didn't want to kill him. That was Chesley. I was still on the rope when he shot him. The lights were out. I thought he had gone to bed."

Small faded away into the half-light, slurring his words and falling finally into unconsciousness as the ambulance arrived. When they shoved his body up into the compartment, the blood had dried, and was purple against the wood of his leg.

In a strange way, it was like standing at the gravestone of some tortured spirit, like Cal from East Of Eden, or The Wild One. I was thinking about this quote from Hamann, that Kierkegaard used as an epigram to Fear and Trembling: What Tarquinius Superbus said in the garden, the son understood, but the messenger did not.

CHAPTER EIGHTEEN

It was a few mornings later. There was a fairly well orchestrated manhunt for Chesley Alford, but neither he nor the collection was found. I had taken Beverly to the airport, kissed her on the cheek, and watched her plane take off again for Baltimore. She was going to pack up her stuff, give her boss two weeks notice, and then I would fly up to Baltimore where we would eat crabs with Old Bay seasoning at Annapolis, go to the diner from the Barry Levinson movies, rent a Uhaul, and drive back down to New Orleans, where we would get married, have kids, buy a Chevrolet, eat hot dogs, go to baseball games, and sing American Pie every Memorial Day weekend and Fourth of July.

I was watching the Today Show where Katie Couric was interviewing someone about something or other. She was wearing a red outfit that matched her lipstick, and her hair was purposely unkempt. Bryant Gumbel then did a piece on the O.J. Simpson trial. He was saying something condescending to a jury consultant, as they cut to Al Roker for the weather outside. Putting that show back in Studio 1-A was one of the worst decisions NBC ever made. There was always a couple from Tennessee who went to see a Broadway production of Oklahoma who just couldn't say enough about New York. Al was talking to a singing group from Massachusetts, while a guy in the background was holding a sign which said KATIE WILL YOU MARRY ME?

I needed to get some milk at the grocery store, I realized, as I was fixing my coffee. I was going to buy some fish for dinner, and some artichoke, and corn. The phone rang, and I thought it was the morning conference call from Allison. But it was Edmund. He told me that he had something very important to tell me, and that he would pick me up after the show.

It was a typical day in the check-out line at the uptown Superstore. There's a fat woman next to me with a kid stuck in the top of her basket. She's pulling on the kid's arms but can't get him out. She's got about fifty bucks in food stamps, and she's buying seven bags of Cheetos, four cans of pork and beans, three packs of hot dogs, a case of Check soda, and four cases of I don't even know what it is – they're like these little plastic balls of juice or something, that must be cheap, because people always buy cases of the stuff with food stamps. So you got that. Then you got a rich bitch in her leather mini-skirt, with the two-carat rock on her finger, and she is trying to use her VISA Gold Card in the express lane to buy a carton of milk and a Cosmopolitan magazine. Then you got the old lady dying of emphysema, coughing and hacking, digging through her pocket-book for her last two dollars – she's got a dollar bill, all crumpled up, and two quarters, a nickel, and forty-five pennies, that she counts, one by one, and then the check-out girl counts them again, one by one- so that she can buy a pack of cigarettes, which is just about the last thing in the world that this woman needs. So you finally get to the front of the line. And you write a check, and it's like eight dollars. But they need your name, your driver's license, your date of birth, your home phone, your work phone. If you try to expedite the process, and write it on the check yourself, then they just find something else that they need.

You write the phone number, they need the driver's license. You write the driver's license, they need a date of birth. You write the date of birth, they need work phone and color of hair. It's ridiculous. It's like, 'Listen lady, if I am gonna go to the trouble of stealing somebody's checkbook, I'm not gonna come to the Winn Dixie and buy fruit with it.' That's how I started the show. "Come on, vent your frustrations" I told them. "Brown, from Chalmette, you're on the air."

"Yeah I'm callin about those lawyers you had on the other day."

"Yeah."

"Yeah, I got into a wreck a few months ago. And it was clearly the other guy's fault. I mean he got the ticket and everything. So they take my car to the shop, and say it's gonna cost around two thousand. So I tell the insurance company, and they say okay. Bout a month goes by, and nothin happens. So I call them up, and I say what's goin on, and they give me the run-around, so I say, look, you got one month. I got no pain right now, but I need my car, and if you don't fix it, I might just have to start feelin like I got a little whip-lash, you know? So a month goes by, and I go to a lawyer friend I got in one of those big firms, and he writes a letter, and bam, I get a check for four thousand bucks. And everyone comes up and says it's people like me, people like me. But it aint people like me. It's companies like them. They got accident reports, eye witness reports, tickets, statements, I give them every warning. They pay me what they owe me, it costs them two thousand bucks. But because they jerk me around, it cost em four. And I don't feel guilty. Screw em."

"Can't disagree with you, Brown, it's a problem. Monica, from Metairie, you're on the air."

"Hey Bobby, love the show."

"Thanks. I appreciate it."

"I know exactly what you're saying" she said. "I can remember when they didn't even look at checks unless they were for more than twenty-five dollars, and they didn't check credit cards unless they were more than fifty. Now you write a three dollar check and they have to run it through the computer."

"I know, it's ridiculous."

"Anyway, the reason why I'm calling is to complain about the fast food places. I just went to Burger King with my daughter. All I wanted was two large diet cokes. So they woman comes on. *I, elo elcom to ur-king, ooo ike uuu our ies?* What? *I, elo elcom to ur-king, ooo ike uuu our ies?* I said, no, just two large diet cokes please. She says *uuu.* I said, two diet cokes. *Uuuu.* Two, large, diet, cokes, please. *Eee rive up.* So I go to the window, and I'm thinking to myself, at least there is no way to screw up this order, it's so simple, and sure enough, the woman takes my money, gives me the change, and hands me two large fries."

"Well, really, in all fairness, you should know better. That's like assumption of risk. If you go to the drive-thru, you know that you are heading for trouble. And you've just gotta be prepared to suffer the consequences."

"I know, you're right Bobby. I've learned my lesson. I'm reformed."

"Nice talking to you. Thanks for the call. Hansel, from Midtown, you're on WWL."

"Hey. I'm wondering about the ice that they have in a lot of restaurants in the urinals. You know what I'm talking about Bobby? What's up with that?"

"That's a very good question, Hansel. I'm glad you called. There has been some debate in various circles concerning this tradition, and I think the commonly accepted theory is that it prevents undesirable accumulation by washing the fluid away quite naturally after people have become too drunk or too disgusted to flush the urinal."

"That makes sense" he said. "Thanks."

"Thanks for the call. Brigid, from Slidell, you're on the air."

"Hey Bobby."

"Are you named after Brigitta, from the Sound of Music?"

"No, I'm named after the Matron Saint of Ireland."

"Saint Patrick?"

"No, she's another one."

"Saint Patrick is the one that drove out all the snakes, right?"

"Yeah."

"Well who did you drive out, the Protestants?"

"No, I healed somebody or something."

"Oh. What can I do you for?"

"What you need" she said, "is self-service. Like they have at gas stations. Where they have replaced all of these gas station attendants with automatic credit card machines. You know what I'm talking about? It's a godsend."

"Yeah, wait a second, I wanna talk about this for a minute. Because this is something I feel very strongly about. And I am the first one to admit that I purposely look for the gas stations that are automated, because they are fast, and convenient, and everything that you just said. And I am a selfish impatient bastard. But, at the same time, you have to think about, from an objective point of view, how many jobs that is. Think about how many service stations there are. And these are unskilled jobs. Which are exactly the kind of jobs that we need more of. And this is really the way of the future. And it's only gonna get worse.

The fact is, you don't need two hundred and fifty million people to provide goods and services for two hundred and fifty million people. And we are getting more and more efficient all the time. It's like in the movie Wall Street, when Martin Sheen says that the problem is that we have too few people producing things, and too many people that just live off the buying and selling of others. And I always thought, that's the last thing we need, is more things. We have too many things. And most of it is just a bunch of crap. And but the Republicans, nevertheless, keep pointing to anecdotes, of modern-day Horatio Alger stories, like Rush Limbaugh with all of his Danny's Bake Sales and Lefty & Lorado's Salsa, which are basically just anomalies. And say, see, he did it. You can do it too. And if you don't, it's your own fault, so don't come crying to me. But the truth of the matter is that it isn't their fault. There are thousands of people who have graduated from college, from business schools, from law schools, and even medical schools, who can't find jobs. They want to work, they're able to work, but there just isn't anything left for them to do. And on the other side, the Democrats, they just keep saying that we need to help them, we need to support them, we need to educate them, and put them into a position where they can provide for themselves. But that's just not going to happen. Not just because a lot of them are lazy, and don't want to work, or uneducated, but because there is just no place left for them in our economy. So you can't just keep going with more broad-based programs. Because they made sense in the nineteen fifties when you had ninety percent of the population working, and it made sense to support, or at least help out, the other ten. But you can't have twenty percent of the population supporting the other eighty. Which is what we are eventually coming to. And the ratio is shifting day by day. You have less and less people putting into the system and more and more taking out. And a lot of it is psychological. It's like the chicken and the egg kind of thing. Because why would you waste the time to educate yourself, to go to college, or to graduate school, or even to finish high school, if there isn't going to be a job for you when you get through? Because we can produce so much more than we could ever possibly consume.

Edmund picked me up after the show, and we drove out to the lakefront, where the sun was falling among the clouds and bringing an orange and red warmth to the sky.

He would not tell me what he wanted to show me. He wanted it to be a surprise.

As we pulled into the parking lot beside the marina, I asked him if one of his associates had discovered the treasure, or the dead body of Chesley Alford in the swamp. Just be patient, he told me, and asked me about the show. I still wanted to have him on to do a show about private investigating. Compare what he does to Raymond Chandler characters and Sam Spade. There was a great movie recently about a detective in England with Liam Nieson, called Narrow Suspicion or Under Suspicion or something with Suspicion. I saw it on a plane.

Edmund, on the other hand, wanted to talk about Kant's categorical imperatives, the olympic and the chathonic, and the allegory of the cave.

To Hobbes, I was explaining, the universal exists neither inside the mind nor in the world outside, because our representations are individual and distinct. The universals are merely our names and our signs for things, where thought is a symbolic operation, closely linked with speech.

And, like us, the conversation drifted.

We were out on a boat, in the southeastern part of the lake. The sun was still warm on our backs, and the moon was rising over the water in the darkest part of the sky. I could begin to hear the crickets and frogs singing louder, with the sounds of the planes taking off and landing over at Lakefront Airport, and a trace of the car engines out on I-10. Edmund slipped the boat into a lower gear, and we drifted parallel to this beautiful ketch that was anchored to the south. It must have been fifty-two or fifty-four feet long, with a large mizzen mast and a flawless dark green finish over a wooden hull.

"Is that the same ketch we almost hit the other night?" I asked Edmund.

"That's really not important" he said. He handed me a pair of binoculars, and instructed me to look closely upon the boat's deck. I focused on the halyard, and surveyed the cockpit, where there was no one at the wheel. I took a second look at the bow, where the anchorline climbed up to a wooden gunwale, with water dripping down off of the side. I don't see anything, I told him, dropping the binoculars from my face. Edmund told me to look again.

Her body was motionless against the deck beneath the metal shrouds and stays. Her shape was long and graceful. The tones of her muscles were perfect, and her skin was bronzed by the sun. There was a pile of emeralds on her navel, while her arms lay gently at her side.

There was a man on deck. The midget. He was wearing scuba diving gear, with sheets of water dripping from his hair as he removed his snorkel and mask. He leaned, (though it was not far to lean), over Beverly, dropping a few wet emeralds into her lap.

I sat down on the plastic vinyl seat covers, dropping the binoculars at my side. Edmund shifted the engine into gear again, and we started to head back towards town. I was listening attentively, trying to become lost again in the hum of the engines, but I couldn't forget where we were or what I had just seen. I was staring at the moon, which was a little bit pink and unnatural, as the grey sky seemed to beckon the descending night. She was a beautiful girl, I said. "Was she?" Edmund asked. "I hadn't noticed."

Acknowledgments

I would like to thank everyone who assisted me in the creation of this book, particularly David Tyree, Robert Bonsignore, Alan Medvin, Christine Ferguson, Alan Kirshbom, Isaac and Lilian Kirshbom, Mom and Dad, Penny, Elizabeth, and, of course, Karen.

About the Author

Steve Herman was born and raised in New Orleans, Louisiana, where he attended Isidore Newman School. He received a Bachelor of Arts degree from Dartmouth College, where he was awarded Citations of Excellence in the study of Milton and Shakespeare, and won the Eleanor Frost Playwriting Competition with his one-act play, *The Phoenix Sleeps Tonight.* Herman was then named Order of the Coif at Tulane Law School, where he received his Juris Doctor, *Magna Cum Laude,* in 1994. After graduating from Tulane, Herman clerked for Justice Harry T. Lemmon of the Louisiana Supreme Court. He now practices law in New Orleans, with the law firm of Herman, Herman & Katz. His novels, *The Gordian Knot* and *A Day in the Life of Timothy Stone,* the non-fiction collection of essays, *America and the Law: Challenges for the 21st Century,* first published by Austin & Winfield, and his most recent book, *My Life as a Spy,* are all also available from Gravier House Press.

www.ingramcontent.com/pod-product-compliance
Lightning Source LLC
Chambersburg PA
CBHW051925240626
47153CB00004B/1372